'This is wrong.' Aksel's eyes rested on her slender figure and her rose-flushed face. 'You should not have come to Storvhal.'

Mina felt sick as the realisation sank in that he was rejecting her. 'Last night—' she began. But he cut her off.

'Last night was a mistake that I am not going to repeat.'

'Why?'

Mina was unaware of the raw emotion in her voice, and Aksel schooled his features to hide the pang of guilt he felt.

She bit her lip. Her pride demanded that she should accept his rejection and try to salvage a little of her dignity, but she did not understand why he had suddenly backed off. 'Is it because I'm deaf? You desired me when you didn't know about my hearing loss,' she reminded him when he frowned. 'What else am I supposed to blame for your sudden change of heart?'

'My heart was never involved,' he said bluntly. 'Learning of your hearing impairment is not the reason why I can't have sex with you again.'

'Then what *is* the reason?' The frustration Mina had felt as a child when she had first lost her hearing surged through he̶r̶ ̶v̶o̶i̶c̶e̶. She wished she could hear Aksel. It wasn̶'̶t̶ ̶r̶e̶a̶d̶i̶n̶g̶ his lips, but not being ̶a̶b̶l̶e̶ ̶t̶o̶ ̶h̶e̶a̶r̶ ̶made her feel that there was a wi̶

'I can't have an ̶a̶f̶f̶a̶i̶r̶. I am the ruler of Storvhal, and my ̶f̶i̶r̶s̶t̶ ̶d̶u̶t̶y̶ ̶i̶s̶ ̶t̶o̶ my country.'

Chantelle Shaw lives on the Kent coast, five minutes from the sea, and does much of her thinking about the characters in her books while walking on the beach. An avid reader from an early age, her schoolfriends used to hide their books when she visited—but Chantelle would retreat into her own world, and still writes stories in her head all the time.

Chantelle has been blissfully married to her own tall, dark and very patient hero for over twenty years and has six children. She began to read Harlequin Mills & Boon® romances as a teenager, and throughout the years of being a stay-at-home mum to her brood found romantic fiction helped her to stay sane!

Her aim is to write books that provide an element of escapism, fun, and of course romance for the countless women who juggle work and home-life and who need their precious moments of 'me' time. She enjoys reading and writing about strong-willed, feisty women and even stronger-willed sexy heroes. Chantelle is at her happiest when writing. She is particularly inspired while cooking dinner, which unfortunately results in a lot of culinary disasters! She also loves gardening, taking her very badly behaved terrier for walks and eating chocolate (followed by more walking...at least the dog is slim!).

Chantelle is on Facebook and would love you to drop by and say hello.

Recent titles by the same author:

SECRETS OF A POWERFUL MAN
  (The Bond of Brothers)
HIS UNEXPECTED LEGACY
  (The Bond of Brothers)
CAPTIVE IN HIS CASTLE
AT DANTE'S SERVICE

Did you know these are also available as eBooks?
Visit www.millsandboon.co.uk

A NIGHT IN THE PRINCE'S BED

BY
CHANTELLE SHAW

Published in Great Britain 2014
by Mills & Boon, an imprint of Harlequin (UK) Limited,
Eton House, 18-24 Paradise Road, Richmond, Surrey, TW9 1SR

© 2014 Chantelle Shaw

ISBN: 978-0-263-90894-7

A NIGHT IN THE
PRINCE'S BED

CHAPTER ONE

HE WAS HERE. Again.

Mina had told herself that she would not look for him, but as she stepped out from the wings her eyes darted to the audience thronged in the standing area in front of the stage, and her heart gave a jolt when she saw him.

The unique design of Shakespeare's Globe on London's South Bank meant that the actors on stage could see the individual faces of the audience. The theatre was a modern reconstruction of the famous Elizabethan playhouse, an amphitheatre with an open roof, above which the sky was now turning to indigo as dusk gathered. To try to recreate the atmosphere of the original theatre, minimal lighting was used, and without the glare of footlights Mina could clearly see the man's chiselled features; his razor-edged cheekbones and resolute jaw shaded with stubble that exacerbated his raw masculinity.

His mouth was unsmiling, almost stern, yet his lips held a sensual promise that Mina found intriguing. From the stage she could not make out the colour of his eyes, but she noted the lighter streaks in his dark blond hair. He was wearing the same black leather jacket he had worn on the three previous evenings, and he was so devastatingly sexy that Mina could not tear her eyes from him.

She was curious about why he was in the audience

again. It was true that Joshua Hart's directorial debut of William Shakespeare's iconic love story *Romeo and Juliet* had received rave reviews, but why would anyone choose to stand for two and a half hours to watch the same play for three evenings in a row? Maybe he couldn't afford a seat in one of the galleries, she mused. Tickets for the standing area—known as the yard—were inexpensive and popular, providing the best view of the stage and offering a unique sense of intimacy between the audience and the actors.

Mina tried to look away from him, but her head turned in his direction of its own accord, as if she were a puppet and he had pulled one of her strings. He was staring at her, and the intensity of his gaze stole her breath. Everything faded—the audience and the members of the cast on stage with her—and she was only aware of him.

On the periphery of her consciousness Mina became aware of the lengthening silence. She sensed the growing tension of the actors around her and realised that they were waiting for her to speak. Her mind went blank. She stared at the audience and sickening fear churned in her stomach as she registered the hundreds of pairs of eyes staring back at her.

Oh, God! Stage-fright was an actor's worst nightmare. Her tongue was stuck to the roof of her mouth and sweat beaded on her brow. Instinctively she raised her hands to her ears to check that her hearing aids were in place.

'*Focus,* Mina!' A fierce whisper from one of the other actors dragged her from the brink of panic. Her brain clicked into gear and, snatching a breath, she delivered her first line.

'"How now, who calls?"'

Kat Nichols, who was playing the role of Nurse, let out an audible sigh of relief.

"'Your mother.'"

"'Madam, I am here. What is your will?'"

The actress playing Lady Capulet stepped forward to speak her lines, and the conversation between Lady Capulet and the Nurse allowed Mina a few seconds to compose herself. Her hesitation had been brief and she prayed that the audience had been unaware of her lapse in concentration. But Joshua would not have missed it. The play's director was standing in the wings and even without glancing at him Mina sensed his irritation. Joshua Hart demanded perfection from every member of the cast, but especially from his daughter.

Mina knew she had ignored one of acting's golden rules when she had broken the 'fourth wall'—the imaginary wall between the actors on stage and the audience. For a few moments she had stepped out of character of the teenage Juliet and given the audience a glimpse of her true self—Mina Hart, a twenty-five year-old partially deaf actress.

It was unlikely that anyone in the audience was aware of her hearing impairment. Few people outside the circle of her family and close friends knew that as a result of contracting meningitis when she was eight she had been left with serious hearing loss. The digital hearing aids she wore were small enough to fit discreetly inside her ears and were hidden by her long hair. The latest designed aids enabled her to have a telephone conversation and listen to music. Sometimes she could almost forget how lonely and cut off she had felt as a deaf child who had struggled to cope in a world that overnight had become silent.

Although Mina had complete confidence in her hearing aids, old habits remained. She was an expert at lip-reading and from instinct rather than necessity she watched Lady Capulet's lips move as she spoke.

"'Tell me, daughter Juliet, how stands your dispositions to be married?'"

The exquisite poetry of Shakespeare's prose was music to Mina's ears and touched her soul. Reality slipped away. She was not an actress, she *was* Juliet, a maid of not yet fourteen who was expected to marry a man of her parents' choosing, a girl on the brink of womanhood who was not free to fall in love, unaware that by the end of the night she would have lost her heart irrevocably to Romeo.

Speaking in a clear voice, Juliet replied to her mother.

"'It is an honour that I dream not of.'"

The play continued without further hitches, but in one corner of her mind Mina was aware that the man in the audience didn't take his eyes off her.

Shakespeare's tale of star-crossed lovers was drawing to its tragic conclusion. After standing for more than two hours, Prince Aksel Thoresen's legs were beginning to ache, but he barely registered the discomfort. His eyes were riveted on the stage, as Juliet, kneeling by her dead husband Romeo, picked up a dagger and plunged the blade into her heart.

A collective sigh from the audience rippled around the theatre like a mournful breeze. Everyone knew how the ill-fated love story ended, but as Juliet's lifeless form slumped across the body of her lover Aksel felt a sudden constriction in his throat. All the members of the cast were skilled actors, but Mina Hart, who played Juliet, was outstanding. Her vivid and emotive portrayal of a young woman falling in love was electrifying.

Aksel's decision to visit Shakespeare's Globe three nights ago had been at the end of another frustrating day of discussions between the governing council of Storvhal and British government ministers. Storvhal was a princi-

pality stretching above Norway and Russia in the Arctic
Circle. The country had been governed by the Thoresen
royal dynasty for eight hundred years, and Aksel, as monarch and head of state, had supreme authority over his
elected council of government. It was a position of great
privilege and responsibility that he had shouldered since
the death of his father, Prince Geir. He had never admitted to anyone that sometimes the role that had been his
destiny from birth felt like a burden.

His visit to London had been to discuss proposals for
a new trade agreement between Britain and Storvhal,
but negotiations had been hampered by endless red tape.
A trip to the theatre had seemed a good way to unwind,
away from the rounds of diplomatic talks. He had certainly not expected that he would develop a fascination
with the play's leading actress.

The play ended, and as the actors walked onto the
stage and bowed to the audience Aksel could not tear his
eyes from Mina. This was the last evening that the play
would be performed at the Globe. It was also his last night
in London. Having finally secured a trade agreement
with the UK, tomorrow he was returning to Storvhal and
his royal duties, which, as his grandmother constantly reminded him, meant that he must choose a suitable bride
to be his princess and produce an heir.

'It is your duty to ensure the continuation of the Thoresen royal dynasty,' Princess Eldrun had insisted in
a surprisingly fierce voice for a woman of ninety who
had recently been seriously ill with pneumonia. 'It is my
greatest wish to see you married before I die.'

Emotional blackmail from anyone else would have left
Aksel unmoved. From childhood it had been impressed
on him that duty and responsibility took precedence over
his personal feelings. Only once had he allowed his heart

to rule his head. He had been in his twenties when he had fallen in love with a beautiful Russian model, but the discovery that Karena had betrayed him was only one of the reasons why he had built an impenetrable wall around his emotions.

His grandmother was the single chink in his armour. Princess Eldrun had helped her husband, Prince Fredrik, to rule Storvhal for fifty years and Aksel had immense respect for her. When she had fallen ill and the doctors had warned him to prepare for the worst he had realised just how much he valued her wise counsel. But even for his grandmother's sake Aksel was not going to rush into marriage. He would choose a bride when he was ready, but it would not be a love match. Being Prince of Storvhal allowed Aksel many privileges but falling in love was not one of them, just as it had not been for his Viking ancestors.

Perhaps it was the knowledge that his grandmother's health was failing that had caused his uncharacteristic emotional response to the tragedy of *Romeo and Juliet*, he brooded. Today was the twelfth anniversary of when his father had been killed in a helicopter crash in Monaco—the playground of the rich and famous where Prince Geir had spent most of his time—to the dismay of the Storvhalian people. In contrast to his father Aksel had devoted himself to affairs of state and slowly won back support for the monarchy, but his popularity came with a price.

In Storvhal he could rarely escape the limelight. The media watched him closely, determined to report any sign of him becoming a party-loving playboy as his father had been. There would be no opportunities for him to go out alone as he had been able to do in London. If he went to the theatre he would have to sit in the royal box, in full view of everyone in the auditorium. He would not be able to stand unrecognised in a crowd and be moved almost to tears by the greatest love story ever told.

He stared at Mina Hart. The cast wore Renaissance costumes and she was dressed in a simple white gown made of gauzy material that skimmed her slender figure. Her long auburn hair framed her heart-shaped face and she looked innocent yet sensual. Aksel felt his body tauten with desire. For a moment he allowed himself to imagine what might happen if he were free to pursue her. But the inescapable truth was that his life was bound by duty. For the past three evenings he had escaped to a fantasy world, but now he must step back to reality.

This was the last time he would see Mina. He studied her face as if he could imprint her features on his memory, and felt a curious ache in his chest as he murmured beneath his breath, 'Goodbye, sweet Juliet.'

'Are you coming for a drink?' Kat Nichols asked as she followed Mina out of the theatre. 'Everyone's meeting up at the Riverside Arms to celebrate the play's successful run.'

Mina had planned to go straight home after the evening performance but she changed her mind when Kat gave a persuasive smile. 'Okay, I'll come for one drink. It's strange to think that we won't be appearing at the Globe any more.'

'But maybe we'll be appearing on Broadway soon.' Kat gave Mina a sideways glance as they walked the short distance to the pub. 'Everyone knows that your father has been in negotiations to take the production to New York. Has he said anything to you about what's going to happen?'

Mina shook her head. 'I know everyone thinks Joshua confides in me because I'm his daughter, but he doesn't treat me any differently from the rest of the cast. I had to audition three times for the role of Juliet. Dad doesn't give me any special favours.'

If anything, her father was tougher on her than other members of the cast, Mina thought ruefully. Joshua Hart was himself a brilliant actor, and a demanding perfectionist. He was not the easiest man to get on with, and Mina's relationship with him had been strained since the events that had happened while she had been filming in America had led Joshua to accuse her of bringing the Hart name into disrepute.

Kat was not deterred. 'Just imagine if we do appear on Broadway! It would be a fantastic career opportunity. You never know, we might even get spotted by a top film director and whisked off to LA.'

'Take it from me, LA isn't so wonderful,' Mina said drily.

Kat gave her a close look. 'I've heard rumours, but what did actually happen when you went to America to make a film?'

Mina hesitated. She had become good friends with Kat, but even so she could not bear to talk about the darkest period of her life. Her memories of the film director Dexter Price were still painful two years after their relationship had ended in a storm of newspaper headlines. She couldn't believe she had been such a gullible fool to have fallen in love with Dex, but she had been alone in LA for her first major film role—young, naïve, and desperately insecure about her hearing impairment. The American film industry demanded perfection, and she had felt acutely conscious of her disability.

She had been grateful for Dexter's reassurance, and within a short time she had fallen for his blend of sophistication and easy charm. Looking back, Mina wondered if one reason why she had been drawn to Dex was because he had reminded her of her father. Both were powerful men who were highly regarded in the acting world, and Dex had given her the support she had always craved from Joshua Hart. When Mina had found out that Dex had lied to her it was not only his betrayal that had left her heartbroken, but the fact that once again her father had failed to support her when she had needed him.

'Mina?'

Kat's voice jolted Mina from her thoughts. She gave her friend an apologetic smile as they reached the pub and she opened the door. 'I'll tell you about it another time.'

The pub was busy and fortunately the din of voices was too loud for Kat to pursue the subject. Mina spotted some of the play's cast sitting at a nearby table. 'I'll get the first round,' she told Kat. 'Save me a seat.'

As she fought her way to the bar Mina decided she would have one drink and then leave. The noisy pub made her feel disorientated and she longed for the peace and quiet of her flat. She suspected that there were a few journalists amongst the crowd. Rumours that Joshua Hart's production of *Romeo and Juliet* might go to New York were circulating, and for the past week the paparazzi had been hanging about the theatre hoping for a scoop.

Mina squeezed through the crowd of people gathered in front of the bar and tried to catch the barman's eye. 'Excuse me!'

The barman walked straight past her and she wondered if he hadn't heard her. The loud background noise inside the pub made it difficult for her to hear her own voice and so regulate how loud or softly she spoke. Moments later the same thing happened again when another barman ignored her and went to serve someone else. It was situations like this that made her conscious of her hearing impairment. Her hearing aids worked incredibly well, but as the bar staff continued to take no notice of her she felt a resurgence of her old insecurities about her deafness. She felt invisible, even though she could see herself in the mirror behind the bar.

As she watched her reflection a figure appeared at her shoulder. Mina tensed as she met his gaze in the mirror and her heart slammed against her ribs as she recognised him. It was *him*—the man who had been in the audience—and close up he was even more gorgeous than she'd thought when she had seen him from the stage.

His eyes were a brilliant topaz-blue, glittering like gemstones beneath his well-defined brows that were a shade darker than his streaked blond hair. When Mina had seen him at the theatre the firm line of his mouth had looked forbidding, but as she watched him in the mirror he gave her a smoulderingly sexy smile that made her catch her breath.

'Perhaps I can be of assistance?'

The gravelly huskiness of his voice caused the tiny hairs on the back of Mina's neck to stand on end. She could not place his accent. Slowly she turned to face him, conscious that her pulse was racing.

'One advantage of my height is that I can usually attract the attention of bar staff,' he murmured. 'Can I buy you a drink?'

His stunning looks and sheer magnetism ensured that he would *never* be ignored. Mina flushed when she realised that she was staring at him. 'Actually, I'm trying to order drinks for my friends…but thanks for the offer.'

Her voice trailed off as her eyes locked with his. She could feel the vibration of her blood pounding in her ears as she studied his lean, handsome face. He was ruggedly male and utterly beautiful. Was this how Juliet had felt when she had first set eyes on Romeo? Mina wondered. In her character study of the role of Juliet she had tried to imagine how it felt to be a teenage girl who had fallen desperately in love at first sight with a young man. It had been more difficult than Mina had expected to step into Juliet's shoes. Could you really feel such intense emotion for someone you had just met, before you had got to know them?

Her common sense had rejected the idea. The story of *Romeo and Juliet* was just a fantasy. But now, in a heartbeat, Mina understood that it was possible to feel an overwhelming connection with a stranger. Even more startling was her certainty that the man felt it too. His eyes narrowed on her face and his body tensed like a jungle cat watching its prey.

Someone pushed past her on their way to the bar and knocked her against the stranger. Her breasts brushed his chest and an electrical current shot through her. Every nerve ending tingled and her nipples instantly hardened and throbbed. For a few seconds she felt dizzy as the heat of his body and the spicy scent of his aftershave hijacked her senses and filled her with a fierce yearning that pooled hot and molten in the pit of her stomach.

With a little gasp she jerked away from him. He was watching her intently, as if he could read her mind. In a desperate attempt to return to normality, she blurted out, 'You were at the theatre tonight. I saw you. Did you enjoy the play?'

His bright blue eyes burned into her. '*You* were— astonishing.'

He spoke in a low, intense voice, and Mina was startled to see colour flare briefly along his sharp cheekbones. She had the impression that he had intended to make a casual response to her question but the words had escaped his lips before he could prevent them.

Thinking about his lips was fatal. Her eyes focused on the sensual curve of his mouth and her breath caught in her throat.

'You came last night, too…and the night before that,' she said huskily.

'I couldn't keep away.' He stared deeply into her eyes, trapping her with his sensual magic so that Mina could not look away from him. Weakness washed over her and butterflies fluttered in her stomach. She swayed towards him, unable to control her body's response to the invisible lure of male pheromones and sizzling sexual chemistry.

A bemused expression crossed the man's face and he shook his head as if he was trying to snap back to reality. He pulled a hand through his dark blond hair, raking it back from his brow.

'Tell me what your friends want to drink and I'll place your order.'

Friends? The spell broke and Mina glanced around the busy pub. Somehow she gathered her thoughts and reeled off a list of drinks. The stranger had no trouble catching the attention of the bar staff and minutes later Mina paid for the round and wondered how she was going to carry a tray of drinks across the crowded room.

Once again the stranger came to her rescue and picked up the tray. 'I'll carry this. Show me where your friends are sitting.'

Kat's eyes widened when she spotted Mina approaching the table followed by a tall, fair-haired man who resembled a Viking. The stranger put the tray of drinks down on the table and Mina wondered if she should invite him to join her and her friends. She wished Kat would stop staring at him.

'Thanks for your help. I'm Mina, by the way.' Worried that she might not hear him in the noisy pub, she watched his mouth closely so that she could read his lips.

Amusement flashed in his blue eyes. 'I know. Your name was on the theatre programme.' He held out his hand. 'I'm Aksel.'

'That's not an English name,' Mina murmured, trying not to think about the firm grip of his fingers as she placed her hand in his. The touch of his skin on hers sent a tingling sensation up her arm and she felt strangely reluctant to withdraw her hand again.

He hesitated fractionally before replying, 'You're right. I am from Storvhal.'

'That's near Russia, isn't it—in the Arctic Circle?'

His brows lifted. 'I'm impressed. Storvhal is a very small country and most people haven't a clue where it is.'

'I'm addicted to playing general knowledge quizzes,' Mina admitted. 'The location of Storvhal often comes up.'

God, did that make her sound like a boring nerd who spent a lot of time on her own? People often assumed that actors led exciting and glamorous lives, but that was far from the truth, Mina thought wryly. There had been plenty of times when she'd been between acting roles and had to take cleaning jobs or stack shelves in a supermarket. Most actors, unless they made it big in the American film industry, struggled to earn a good living. But Mina was not driven by money and had been drawn to the stage because acting was in her blood.

The Harts were a renowned theatrical family, headed by Joshua Hart, who was regarded as the greatest Shakespearean actor of the past thirty years. Mina had wanted to be an actress since she was a small child and she had refused to allow her hearing loss to destroy her dream.

But the dream had turned sour in LA. Making a film there had been an eye-opener and she had hated the celebrity culture, the gossip and backbiting. The events in LA had had a profound effect on her and when she had returned to England she had re-evaluated what she wanted to do with her life, and she had recently qualified as a drama therapist.

One thing she was certain of was that she never wanted her private life to be splashed across the front pages of the tabloids ever again. It still made her shudder when she remembered the humiliation of reading explicit and inaccurate details about her relationship with Dexter Price in the newspapers. The paparazzi did not seem to care about reporting the truth, and Mina had been a target of their ruthless desire for scandal. She had developed a deep mistrust of the press—and in particular of the man she had just spotted entering the pub.

She froze when she recognised him. Steve Garratt was the journalist who had exposed her affair with Dexter. Garratt had written a scurrilous article in which he had accused Mina of sleeping with the film director to further her career while Dexter's wife had been undergoing treatment for cancer. Most of the article had been untrue. Mina had never been to bed with Dex—although she had been in love with him, and ready to take the next step in their relationship, before she had discovered that he was married. But no one had been interested in her side of the story, certainly not Steve Garratt.

What was Garratt doing here in the UK? It was unlikely to be a coincidence that he had turned up at the same time as rumours were rife that Joshua Hart's production of *Romeo and Juliet* might be performed on Broadway. Garratt was after a story and Mina's heart sank when the journalist looked over in her direction and gave her a cocky smile of recognition.

As he began to thread his way across the pub she felt a surge of panic. She could not bear the embarrassment of the journalist talking about the LA scandal in front of her friends from the theatre company. The story had been mostly forgotten after two years, and she had hoped it would remain dead and buried.

She glanced at the good-looking man who had introduced himself as Aksel. They were strangers, she reminded herself. The curious connection she felt with him must be a figment of her imagination.

'Well, it was nice to meet you,' she murmured. 'Thanks for your help.'

Aksel realised he was being dismissed. It was a novel experience for a prince and in different circumstances he might have been amused, but inexplicably he felt a rush of jealousy when he noticed that Mina was staring at a man who had just entered the pub. Was the man her boyfriend? It was of no interest to him, he reminded himself. He was regretting his decision to follow Mina into the pub, and her obvious interest in the man who was now approaching them was a signal to Aksel that it was time he left.

'You're welcome.' His eyes met hers, and for a split second he felt a crazy urge to grab hold of her hand and whisk her away from the crowded pub to somewhere they could be alone.

What the hell had got into him tonight? he asked himself irritably. His behaviour was completely out of character and he must end his ridiculous fascination with Mina Hart right now. 'Enjoy the rest of your evening,' he bade her curtly, and strode out of the pub without glancing back at her.

* * *

'Mina Hart, what a pleasant surprise!' Steve Garratt drawled. He smelled of stale cigarette smoke and Mina wrinkled her nose as he leaned too close to her.

'I find nothing pleasant about meeting you,' she said coldly. 'And I doubt you're surprised to see me. You're here for a reason, and I can guess what it is.'

The journalist grinned to reveal nicotine-stained teeth. It was warm inside the pub and his florid face was turning pinker. 'A little bird told me you'll soon be making your Broadway debut.'

'Who told you that?' Mina asked sharply. She glanced at his shifty expression and realised that he was hoping to goad her into giving him information.

'Come on, sweetheart. Everyone wants to know if your father will be directing *Romeo and Juliet* in New York. He must have told you whether it's going to happen. All the hacks are hoping to break the story. Give me an exclusive and I'll make sure you get good reviews if you do open on Broadway.'

'Joshua hasn't told me anything, but even if he had confided in me I wouldn't tell you. You're a weasel, Garratt. You nose around in people's private lives looking for scandal and if none exist you make up lies—like you did to me.' Mina broke off, breathing hard as she struggled to control her temper.

The journalist gave a cynical laugh. 'Am I supposed to feel sorry for you? Don't give me that bull about journalists respecting celebrities' private lives. Actors need publicity. You don't really believe that a film starring an unknown English actress would have been a box-office success on its own merits, do you? People went to see *Girl in the Mirror* because they were curious about the bimbo who screwed Dexter Price.'

Steve Garratt's mocking words made Mina's stomach churn. The pub felt claustrophobic and she was suddenly desperate for some fresh air. She pushed past the journalist, unable to bear being in his company for another second. 'You disgust me,' she told him bitterly.

Kat was chatting with the other members of the cast and Mina did not interrupt them. They would guess she had gone home, she told herself as she made her way across the crowded pub towards the door. Outside, it was dark. The October nights were drawing in and Mina's lightweight jacket did not offer much protection against the chilly wind. Head bowed, she walked briskly along the pavement that ran alongside the river. The reflection of the street lights made golden orbs on the black water, but soon she turned off the well-lit main road down a narrow alleyway that provided the quickest route to the tube station.

Her footsteps echoed loudly in the enclosed space. It wasn't late, but there was no one around, except for a gang of youths who were loitering at the other end of the alleyway. From the sound of their raucous voices Mina guessed they had been drinking. She thought about turning back and going the long route to the station, but she was tired and, having grown up in central London, she considered herself fairly streetwise. Keeping her head down, she continued walking, but as she drew nearer to the gang she noticed they were passing something between them and guessed it was a joint.

Her warning instincts flared. Something about the youths' body language told her that they were waiting for her to walk to the far end of the alley. She stopped abruptly and turned round, but as she hurriedly retraced her steps the gang followed her.

'Hey, pretty woman, why don't you want to walk this way?' one of them called out.

Another youth laughed. 'There's a film called *Pretty Woman*, about a slag who makes a living on the streets.' The owner of the voice, a skinhead with a tattoo on his neck, caught up with Mina and stood in front of her so that she was forced to stop walking. 'Is that what you do—sell your body? How much do you charge?' As the gang crowded around Mina the skinhead laughed. 'Do you do a discount for group sex?'

Mina swallowed, trying not to show that she was scared. 'Look, I don't want any trouble.' She took a step forwards and froze when the skinhead gripped her arm. 'Let go of me,' she demanded, sounding more confident than she felt.

'What if I don't want to let go of you?' the skinhead taunted. 'What are you going to do about it?' He slid his hand inside Mina's jacket and she felt a surge of fear and revulsion when he tugged her shirt buttons open. The situation was rapidly spiralling out of control. The youths were drunk, or high—probably both—and on a cold autumn night it was unlikely that anyone was around to help her.

'You'd better let me go. I'm meeting someone, and if I don't show up they'll start looking for me,' she improvised, thinking as she spoke that her friends at the pub would assume she had gone home.

The skinhead must have sensed that she was bluffing. 'So, where's your friend?'

'Here,' said a soft, menacing voice.

Mina's gaze shot to the end of the alleyway that she had entered a few minutes earlier and her heart did a somersault in her chest. The light from the street lamp behind him made his blond hair look like a halo. Surely no angel could be so devastatingly sexy, but to Mina, scared out of her wits, he was her guardian angel, her saviour.

The skinhead, surprised by the interruption, had loosed his grip on her arm, and Mina wrenched herself free.

'Aksel,' she said on a half-sob, and ran towards him.

CHAPTER TWO

'IT'S ALL RIGHT, Mina, you're safe,' Aksel murmured. He felt the tremors that shook her slender frame. When she had raced down the alleyway he had instinctively opened his arms and she had flown into them. He stroked her auburn hair, one part of his brain marvelling at how silky it felt. At the same time he eyed the gang of youths and felt a cold knot of rage in the pit of his stomach when the skinhead who had been terrorising Mina stepped forwards.

'Can't you count, mate? There's six of us and only one of you,' the gang leader said with a show of bravado.

'True, but I am worth more than the six of you combined,' Aksel drawled in an icy tone that cut through the air like tempered steel. He never lost his temper. A lifetime of controlling his emotions had taught him that anger was far more effective served ice-cold and deadly. 'I'm willing to take you all on.' He flicked his gaze over the gang members. 'But one at a time is fair, man to man—if you've got the guts of real men.'

He gently put Mina to one side and gave her a reassuring smile when her eyes widened in fear as she realised what he intended to do.

'Aksel...you can't fight them all,' she whispered.

He ignored her and strolled towards the skinhead

youth. 'If you're the leader of this pack of sewer rats I guess you'll want to go first.'

The skinhead had to tilt his head to look Aksel in the face, and doubt flickered in his eyes when he realised that his adversary was not only tall but powerfully built. Realising that he was in serious danger of losing face, he spat out a string of crude profanities as he backed up the alleyway. The other youths followed him and Aksel watched them until they reached the far end of the alley and disappeared.

'You have got to be nuts!' Mina sagged against the wall. Reaction to the knowledge that Aksel had saved her from being mugged or worse was setting in and her legs felt wobbly. 'They could have been carrying a weapon. You could have been hurt.'

She stared at him and felt weak for another reason as she studied his chiselled features and dark blond hair that had fallen forwards onto his brow. He raked it back with his hand and gave her a disarming smile that stole her breath.

'I could have handled them.' He frowned as Mina moved and the edges of her jacket parted to reveal her partially open shirt. 'That punk had no right to lay a finger on you. Did he hurt you?' Aksel felt a resurgence of the scalding anger that had gripped him when he had seen the skinhead gang leader seize hold of Mina. A lifetime of practice had made him adept at controlling his emotions, but when he had seen her scared face as the gang of youths crowded round her he had been filled with a murderous rage.

'No, I'm fine. *Oh...*' Mina coloured hotly as she glanced down and saw that her shirt was half open, exposing her lacy bra and the upper slopes of her breasts. She fumbled to refasten the buttons with trembling fingers. Nausea swept over her as her vivid imagination pictured what the gang of youths might have done to her if Aksel had not shown up.

'Thank you for coming to my rescue—again,' she said shakily, remembering how he had helped her order drinks at the bar earlier. The memory of how she had thrown herself into his arms when he had appeared in the alley brought another stain of colour to her cheeks. 'By the way, I'm sorry I behaved like an idiot and hugged you.'

His lips twitched. 'No problem. Feel free to hug me any time you like.'

'Oh,' Mina said again on a whispery breath that did not sound like her normal voice. But nothing about this evening was normal, and it was not surprising she felt breathless when Aksel was looking at her in a way that made her think he was remembering those few moments when he had caught her in his arms and held her so close to him that her breasts had been squashed against his chest.

Keen to move on from that embarrassing moment, she quickly changed the subject. 'What are you doing here?'

Aksel had been asking himself the same question since he had left the Globe Theatre after the performance. His car had been waiting for him, but as his chauffeur had opened the door he'd felt a surge of rebellion against the constrictions of his life. He knew that back at his hotel his council members who had accompanied him from Storvhal would be waiting to discuss the new trade deal. But Aksel's mind had been full of the Shakespearean tragedy that had stirred his soul, and the prospect of spending the rest of the evening discussing politics had seemed unendurable.

No doubt Harald Petersen, his elderly chief advisor and close friend of his grandmother, would be critical of the fact that he had dismissed his driver and bodyguard.

'I am sure I don't need to remind you that Storvhal's wealth and political importance in the world are growing, and there is an increased risk to your personal safety, sir,' Harald had said when Aksel had argued against the necessity of being accompanied by a bodyguard while he was in London.

'I think it's unlikely that I'd be recognised anywhere other than in my own country,' Aksel had pointed out. 'I've always kept a low media profile at home and abroad.' Unlike his father, whose dubious business dealings and playboy lifestyle had often made headlines around the world.

After he had sent his driver away, Aksel had strolled beside the river when he had spotted Mina entering a pub, and without stopping to question what he was doing he had followed her inside. His immediate thought when he had met her at the bar was that, close up, she was even more beautiful than he'd thought when he had seen her on stage. He'd looked into her deep green eyes and felt as if he were drowning.

'When you left the pub, I assumed I would never see you again.' Her soft voice pulled Aksel back to the alleyway.

'I was about to get into a taxi when I saw you come out of the pub. I watched you turn down this alleyway and decided to follow you. A badly lit alley doesn't seem a good place to walk on your own at night.'

Mina gave him a rueful glance. 'I'm on my way home and this is the quickest way to the station.'

'Why didn't you stay with your friends?' Aksel hesitated. 'You looked over at a man who walked into the pub and I thought he must be someone you knew.'

Aksel must be referring to Steve Garratt. Supressing a shudder, Mina shook her head. 'He was no one—just…a guy.' She swallowed, thinking that the only reason she had left the pub and started to walk to the station alone at night was because she'd wanted to get away from the journalist she despised.

She had a flashback to the terrifying moment when the gang of youths had surrounded her, and the colour drained from her face.

'Are you all right?' Aksel looked at her intently. 'You're in shock. Do you feel faint?'

Mina was not going to admit that she felt close to tears. 'I probably feel wobbly because I'm hungry. I'm always too nervous to eat before a performance,' she explained ruefully. 'That's why I was going home to get something to eat.'

His sensual smile evoked a coiling sensation in the pit of Mina's stomach.

'I have an idea. Why don't you have dinner with me? My hotel isn't far from here, and it has an excellent restaurant. I'm sure you won't feel like cooking a meal when you get home,' he said persuasively.

'I...I couldn't impose on you any further.' For a crazy moment she wanted to accept Aksel's invitation. It would be madness, she told herself. He was a stranger she had met in a pub and she knew nothing about him other than that he came from a country most people had never heard of. She looked at him curiously. 'Are you on holiday in England?'

'A business trip—I'm flying home tomorrow.'

She crushed her ridiculous feeling of disappointment. 'What line of business are you in?'

Was it her imagination, or did an awkward expression flit across his face before he replied? 'I work as an advisor for my country's government. My visit to London was with a delegation to discuss trade policies with Britain.'

Mina could not hide her surprise. With his streaked blond hair and leather jacket he looked more like a rock star than a government advisor. 'It sounds interesting,' she murmured.

His laughter echoed through the alleyway; a warm, mellow sound that melted Mina's insides. 'I would have expected an actress to be more convincing at pretending that my job sounds fascinating,' he said softly. 'Can I persuade you to have dinner with me if I promise I won't bore you with details about trade policies?'

As she met his glinting, bright blue gaze Mina thought it would be impossible for Aksel to bore her. Her common sense told her to walk back out to the main street and hail a taxi to take her home. She would be mad to go to dinner with a stranger, even if he was the sexiest man she had ever laid eyes on. She had followed her heart in LA but her experience with Dexter Price had left her wary and mistrustful, not just of other men but of her own judgement.

'I'm not dressed for dinner at a restaurant.' She made another attempt to ignore the voice of temptation that was telling her to throw caution to the wind and go with Aksel. Besides, it was the truth. Her cotton gypsy skirt and cheesecloth shirt were very boho chic, according to Kat, but not a suitable outfit to wear to dinner.

'You look fine to me,' Aksel assured her in his seductive, gravelly voice. 'There's just one thing. You've done your buttons up in the wrong order.'

He moved closer, and Mina caught her breath as he lifted his hands and fastened her shirt buttons properly. He smelled of sandalwood cologne, mingled with a clean, fresh fragrance of soap and another barely discernible scent that was intensely male and caused Mina's stomach muscles to tighten.

As if he sensed her indecision, Aksel gave her another of his sexy smiles that set Mina's pulse racing. 'I understand the hotel restaurant serves a rich chocolate mousse that is utterly decadent. What do you say to us both sampling it this evening?'

His gravelly voice was electrifying, or maybe it was the expression in his eyes as he'd put a subtle emphasis on the word decadent. They both knew he hadn't been thinking about chocolate dessert as he'd said it, and Mina was unable to control the tiny tremor that ran through her.

He frowned. 'You're cold. Here…' Before she could protest he slipped off his leather jacket and draped it around her shoulders. The silk lining was warm from his body and Mina felt a wild, wanton heat steal through her veins. He caught hold of her hand and led her back to the entrance of the alleyway, but then he stopped and glanced down at her, his expression enigmatic.

'I have a taxi waiting. I'll ask the driver to take us to my hotel, or take you home. It's your choice.'

It was crunch time, Mina realised. She sensed that if she chose to go home Aksel would not argue. It would be sensible to refuse his offer of dinner, but a spark of rebellion flared inside her. Since she had returned from LA she had built a shell around herself and stayed firmly inside her comfort zone, afraid to try new experiences. But what harm could there be in agreeing to have dinner with Aksel, who had rescued her from the youths and behaved like a perfect gentleman? Was she going to run a mile from every handsome man she met and allow what had happened with Dexter Price to affect her for the rest of her life?

She hoped he could not tell that butterflies were dancing in her stomach. 'All right, you win. You've seduced me with talk of chocolate mousse, and I'd like to come back to your hotel.'

The moment the words left her lips she realised how suggestive they sounded and colour rushed into her cheeks. 'To have dinner, I meant,' she added quickly. Oh, God, why had she said seduced? She didn't want him to guess that she wished he would kiss her, she thought numbly as her eyes locked with his.

He gave a husky laugh and lowered his head towards her so that his warm breath whispered across her lips. 'I know you meant dinner,' he assured her. His smile was wolfish as he said softly, 'Seduction will come later.'

And then Aksel did what he had wanted to do since he had first set eyes on Juliet three nights ago, what he had ached to do since he had drowned in Mina's deep green gaze when he had met her in the pub. He cupped her face in his hands and brushed his mouth over hers, once, twice, until she parted her lips beneath his.

Mina dissolved instantly when Aksel slanted his mouth over hers. She had fantasised about him kissing her since she had first noticed him in the audience three nights ago, and now fantasy and reality merged in a fire-storm of passion. Her heart pounded as he pulled her hard against him. His body was all powerful muscle and sinew but the heat of his skin through his shirt made her melt into him as he deepened the kiss and it became ach-ingly sensual.

'Oh,' she whispered helplessly as he probed his tongue between her lips. Her little gasp gave Aksel the access he desired, and he slid his hand beneath Mina's hair to cup her nape while he crushed her mouth beneath his. The sweet eagerness of her response drew a ragged groan from him. He could have kissed her for ever, but one part of his brain reminded him that he was a prince and he was breaking every rule of protocol by kissing a woman he barely knew in a public alleyway.

Reluctantly he lifted his mouth from hers. 'Will you come with me, Mina?'

Mina stared into Aksel's eyes that glittered as brightly as the stars she could see winking in the black strip of sky above the alleyway. Her common sense warned her to refuse, but on a deeper instinctive level she knew she would be safe with him. She nodded mutely and followed him out of the alley to the main road where a taxi was waiting.

She couldn't stop looking at him, drinking in the chiselled masculine beauty of his face and his sensual mouth that had wreaked havoc on hers. And he could not stop looking at her. They were both blind to everything around them, and as they climbed into the taxi neither of them noticed the man who had just emerged from the pub and watched them from the shadows before he got into his car and followed the taxi at a discreet distance.

Some time soon his common sense was going to return, Aksel assured himself as he gave the taxi driver the name of his hotel and leaned back against the seat. He glanced at Mina and was shocked by how out of control she made him feel. He wanted to kiss her again. Hell, he wanted to do a lot more than kiss her, he acknowledged derisively. His body throbbed with desire, and only the knowledge that the taxi driver was watching them in the rear-view mirror stopped him from drawing her into his arms and running his hands over the soft contours of her body that she had pressed against him when they had kissed in the alleyway.

The taxi driver's curiosity reminded Aksel that he had not thought things through when he had invited Mina to dinner. Journalists from Storvhal had accompanied the trade delegation to London and they would jump at the chance to report that the prince had entertained a beautiful actress at his hotel. It was the kind of story his enemies would seize on to fuel rumours that he was turning into a playboy like his father had been.

Scandal had followed Prince Geir like a bad smell, Aksel remembered grimly. During his reign there had even been a move by some of the population to overthrow the monarchy. The protest groups had grown quiet since Aksel had become Prince of Storvhal, but he was conscious of the necessity to conduct his private life with absolute discretion.

While he was debating what to do, his phone rang and presented him with a solution to the problem. Aksel knew that his personal assistant was completely trustworthy, and he instructed Benedict to arrange a private dinner for him and a guest.

Mina did not recognise the language Aksel was speaking when he answered his phone, but she guessed it was Storvhalian. It was a more guttural sound than Italian, which she had learned to speak a little when she had spent a month in Sicily with her sister Darcey.

Listening to Aksel talking in an unfamiliar language reminded Mina that she knew nothing about him other than that he worked as some kind of advisor for his government. She had also discovered that he was an amazing kisser, which suggested he'd had plenty of practice at kissing women, she thought ruefully. She glanced at his chiselled profile and acknowledged that with his stunning looks he was likely to be very sexually experienced. Maybe he had a girlfriend in Storvhal. She stiffened as another thought struck her. Maybe he had a wife.

He finished his phone conversation and must have

mistaken the reason for her tension because he said softly, 'Forgive my rudeness. I am used to speaking to my PA in my own language.'

'It's late to be talking to a member of your staff.' Mina hesitated. 'I wondered if it was a girlfriend who called you...or your wife.'

His brows lifted. 'I'm not married. Do you think I would have asked you to dinner—hell, do you think I would have kissed you if I was in a relationship?'

Mina held her ground. 'Some men would.'

'I'm not one of them.'

The quiet implacability of his tone convinced her. Perhaps she was a fool to trust him, but Mina sensed that Aksel had a strong code of honour. He had a curious, almost regal air about him that made her wonder if his role in the Storvhalian government was more important that he had led her to believe. Perhaps he was actually a member of the government rather than an advisor.

But would a government minister have kissed her with such fierce passion? Why not? she mused. Not all politicians were crusty old men. Aksel was an incredibly handsome, sexy, *unmarried* man who was free to kiss her, just as she was free to kiss him. Heat flooded through her as she recalled the firm pressure of his lips on hers, the hunger that had exploded in her belly when he had pushed his tongue into her mouth.

'You spoke as if you have personal experience of the type of man who would cheat on his wife.'

Mina shrugged. 'I was just making a general comment.' She sensed from the assessing look Aksel gave her that he wasn't convinced, but to her relief he did not pursue the subject as the taxi came to a halt outside one of London's most exclusive hotels.

'You didn't say you were staying at The Erskine,' she

muttered, panic creeping into her voice as she watched a doorman dressed in a top hat and tailcoat usher a group of people into the hotel. The men were in tuxedos and the women were all wearing evening gowns. Mina glanced doubtfully at her gypsy skirt and flat ballet pumps. 'I'm definitely not wearing the right clothes for a place like this.'

'I'd forgotten that there's a charity function being held at the hotel this evening.' Aksel frowned as a flashbulb went off and he saw a pack of press photographers outside the hotel, telescopic lenses extended to snap pictures of celebrities attending the event. The last thing he wanted was to be photographed entering the hotel with a beautiful and very noticeable actress. It was the kind of thing that would trigger frantic speculation about his love-life back in Storvhal. He leaned forwards and spoke to the taxi driver, and seconds later the car pulled away from the kerb.

'There's another entrance we can use,' he told Mina. 'I've arranged for us to have dinner privately,' he explained as she slipped his leather jacket from her shoulders and handed it back to him. 'I'm not dressed for a black-tie event either.'

As the taxi turned down a narrow side street Mina checked her phone and read a text message from Kat, reminding her that Joshua Hart had asked the cast to meet at the Globe Theatre at nine a.m. the following day. After quickly texting a reply, she scrambled out of the taxi after Aksel. She stumbled on the uneven pavement and he shot an arm around her waist to steady her. The contact with his body made her catch her breath, and her pulse accelerated when he pulled her close. Keeping his arm around her, Aksel escorted her through an unremarkable-looking door into the hotel. Neither of them noticed the car that had pulled up behind the taxi.

Although they had entered the hotel via a back entrance, they still had to walk across the lobby: an oasis of marble and gold-leaf décor, which this evening was filled with sophisticated guests attending the charity function. Mina felt like a street urchin in her casual clothes and was glad that Aksel whisked her over to the lifts, away from the haughty glances of the reception staff.

As the doors closed she was intensely aware of him in the confined space and her heart lurched when he reached out a hand and brushed her hair back from her face. She tensed. Her hearing aids were tiny but they were fitted into the outer shell of her ears and were visible to someone standing close to her. There seemed no point telling him about her hearing loss when she would not see him again after this evening. He had already told her that he was returning to Storvhal tomorrow. She did not understand why he had asked her to have dinner with him, or why she had agreed, and she suddenly felt out of her depth. What on earth was she doing in a luxurious five-star hotel with a man she did not know?

'What's wrong?' he asked softly. 'If you've changed your mind about dinner I can arrange for you to be taken home.' He paused, and his husky voice sent a shiver across Mina's skin. 'But I hope you'll stay.'

She could feel her blood pounding in her ears, echoing her erratic heartbeat. It terrified her that he had such a devastating effect on her. 'It's ridiculous for two strangers to have dinner,' she blurted out. 'I don't know anything about you.'

'You know that I am a fan of Shakespeare—and chocolate mousse.' His blue eyes glinted as bright as diamonds. 'And I have discovered that you have an incredible talent for acting, and kissing.'

Her breath caught in her throat. 'You shouldn't say that,' she whispered.

'Do you want me to say you're bad at kissing?' His lips twitched with amusement but the expression in his eyes was serious. 'I can't lie, angel, you are amazing, and all I can think of is how much I want to kiss you again.'

Mina did not know if she was relieved or disappointed when the lift stopped and the doors slid smoothly apart. As she followed Aksel along a carpeted corridor the voice of caution inside her head told her to race back to the lift. Her eyes widened when he opened a set of double doors into an exquisitely decorated room where a polished dining table set with silver cutlery and candles reflected the ornate chandelier suspended above it. Vases of oriental lilies placed around the room filled the air with their sweet perfume, and the lamps were dimmed to create an ambiance that was unsettlingly intimate.

Aksel strolled over to the bar and picked up a bottle of champagne from an ice bucket. He popped the cork with a deftness that suggested he was no stranger to champagne, filled two tall flutes and handed one to Mina.

'We'll have a drink while we look at the menu.'

Mina watched his throat move as he swallowed a mouthful of champagne. His dark blond hair had fallen forwards onto his brow again and she longed to run her fingers through it. Conscious that she was staring at him, she took a gulp of her drink and belatedly realised that champagne on an empty stomach was not a good idea. The bubbles hit the back of her throat and seemed to instantly enter her bloodstream, making her head spin.

'Come and sit down.' Aksel draped his jacket over the arm of a sofa and sat down, patting the empty space beside him. He hooked his ankle over his thigh and stretched one arm along the back of the sofa, causing his black silk shirt to strain across his broad chest. He looked indolent and so dangerously sexy that the thought of joining him on the sofa made Mina's heart hammer.

'Um…I'd like to use the bathroom before we eat.'

'The first door on your left along the corridor,' he advised.

Get a grip, Mina told herself sternly a few moments later as she stared at her flushed face in the bathroom mirror. She looked different, more alive, as if a lightbulb had been switched on inside her. Even her hair seemed to crackle with electricity, and her eyes looked enormous, the pupils dilated, reflecting the wild excitement that she could not control. She traced her tongue over her lips, remembering how the firm pressure of Aksel's mouth had forced them apart when he had kissed her.

She held her wrists under the cold tap, hoping to lower her temperature that seemed in danger of boiling over. Maybe if she took her jacket off she would cool down—but the sight of her pebble-hard nipples jutting provocatively beneath her thin shirt put paid to that idea. The jacket would have to stay on. It was better to look hot than desperate!

Oh, hell! Tempting though it was to hide in the bathroom, she had to go out and face him. You're an actress, she reminded herself. You can play cool and collected if you pretend he's in the audience and don't make eye contact with him.

Taking a deep breath, she returned to the dining room and to avoid looking at Aksel she picked up her glass and finished her champagne. He was standing by the window, but turned when she came in and walked towards her.

'I'd love to know what thoughts are going on behind

those mysterious deep green eyes,' he murmured as she swept her long eyelashes down.

'Actually, I was wondering why someone who can afford to stay at a five-star hotel would choose to buy the cheapest ticket at the theatre and stand for a two-hour performance, not just once, but on three evenings. But I suppose,' Mina voiced her thoughts, 'as you are in London on a business trip, your employer would pay for your hotel. You must be very good at your job for your government to put you up at The Erskine.'

Aksel hesitated. Although Mina had heard of Storvhal, she clearly had no idea of his identity, and he did not feel obliged to reveal that he was the ruling monarch of the principality. For one night he wanted to forget his royal responsibilities.

'It's true that my accommodation was arranged for me,' he murmured. 'The first evening when I visited the Globe the only tickets available were for the yard in front of the stage. I probably could have booked a seat in the gallery on the second and third night, but I'll admit I chose to stand so that I had a clear view of you.'

His voice roughened. 'The first time I saw you walk onto the stage you blew me away.'

Mina felt as if the air had been sucked out of her lungs. She understood what he meant because she had felt exactly the same when she had seen him in the audience: utterly blown away by his raw sexuality. Her eyes flew to his face, and the primitive hunger in his gaze mirrored the inexplicable, inescapable need that was flowing like a wild river through her body.

'Aksel…' She had meant it to sound like a remonstration but his name left her lips on a breathy whisper, an invitation, a plea.

'Angel.' He moved towards her, or maybe she moved

first. Mina did not know how she came to be in his arms, only that they felt like bands of steel around her as he pulled her into the hard, warm strength of his body and bent his head to capture her mouth in a kiss that set her on fire.

CHAPTER THREE

MINA REMEMBERED HOW she had run into Aksel's arms when she had fled from the youths in the alleyway. Her instincts had told her she would be safe with him, and she felt that same sense of security now, as if—ridiculous as it seemed—she belonged with him.

He kissed her with increasing passion until she trembled with the intensity of need he was arousing in her. When he eventually lifted his mouth from hers she pressed her lips to his cheek. The blond stubble on his jaw scraped against her skin, heightening her awareness of his raw masculinity. She arched her neck as he traced his lips down her throat, but when he smoothed her hair back behind her ear she quickly turned her head so that he did not see her hearing aids.

He moved his hands over her body, shaping her shoulders, tracing the length of her spine and finally cupping her bottom. She gasped when he jerked her against his pelvis and she felt the unmistakable hard ridge of his arousal. Perhaps she should have felt shocked, or pulled away from him, but she had no control over the molten warmth of her own desire.

'You have no idea how many times in the last three days I have imagined doing this—holding you, kissing you—' Aksel's voice lowered to a husky growl '—making love to you.'

Mina's heart turned over at the thought of where this was leading. Was she really contemplating making love with a man she had only spoken to for the first time a few hours ago? It was madness—and yet hadn't she thought of him constantly since she had spotted him in the audience three nights ago? She had tried to tell herself that she had become too absorbed in the role of Juliet, and had been looking for a real-life Romeo. Fantasising about the blond man in the audience had been just that—a fantasy. But being here with Aksel was real, and so was the urgent, all-consuming desire that was making her heart pound in her chest.

A tiny shred of her sanity still remained and she said almost desperately, 'I don't *do* things like this. I don't go back to strangers' hotels...' She broke off helplessly as he gave her a crooked smile.

'Will you believe that this is a new experience for me too, angel?' Aksel raked his hair back from his brow with an unsteady hand. The restrictions of being a prince meant that he had rarely had the opportunity, and never the inclination, to pick up a woman in a bar. He assured himself that he'd had no ulterior motive when he had invited Mina to his hotel other than that he wanted to get to know her a little better. But the minute they had been alone and he had looked into her deep green eyes his usual restraint had been swept away by a storm surge of desire, and now the situation was rapidly getting out of hand.

'I've never felt like this before,' he admitted rawly. 'I have never wanted any woman as desperately as I want you.'

They were supposed to be having dinner, Aksel reminded himself. Perhaps if they sat down at the table and studied the menu the madness that was making him behave so out of character would pass.

'Are you hungry?'

Aksel spoke in such a low tone that Mina struggled to hear him, but as she watched his lips shape the question she remembered that she had not eaten anything since breakfast. She felt light-headed, probably from the effects of the champagne, she acknowledged ruefully. But hunger seemed to heighten her other senses and evoked a different physical need inside her. Just the thought of Aksel making love to her made her gut twist with desire.

'Yes, I'm hungry,' she replied in a husky, sensual voice that did not sound like her own.

'Do you want to order some food?'

She hesitated for a heartbeat. 'It's not food I want,' she whispered.

He said something in his own language. Mina did not understand the words but the glitter in his eyes was unmistakable as he hauled her against him and brought his mouth down on hers in a kiss that plundered her soul. She did not protest when he lifted her into his arms and strode through a door at the far end of the dining room. With her hands linked at his nape and her face pressed against his throat she was barely aware of her surroundings until he set her on her feet and she saw that they were in a huge bedroom dominated by an enormous bed.

It occurred to her vaguely that he must have a very good job for his country's government to have arranged for him to stay in such a luxurious room. But then he placed his mouth over hers once more and she instantly succumbed to the sensual mastery of his kiss. She was barely aware of him removing her jacket or unbuttoning her shirt and sliding it off her shoulders. Her sheer white bra decorated with tiny lace flowers pushed her breasts high and her dark pink nipples tilted provocatively beneath the semi-transparent material.

Aksel made a harsh sound in his throat as he lifted his hand and traced a finger lightly over her breasts. 'You are even more beautiful than I imagined. You take my breath away.'

Mina's heart gave a jolt as he reached behind her and undid her bra, but she made no attempt to stop him. Not even his ragged groan pierced the mist of unreality that had descended over her, and she gave a little shiver of excitement as her bra cups fell away and her breasts spilled into his palms. She lifted her eyes to his face and saw dull colour streak along his high cheekbones. His reaction to her, the feral glitter in his eyes, made her feel intensely aware of her femininity and her sexual allure. After what had happened with Dexter she had deliberately kept her body hidden beneath shapeless clothes, unwilling to risk attracting any man's attention. But the past and all its humiliating horror seemed far away.

Her sense of unreality deepened. It seemed incredible that her fantasies about the man in the audience were coming true. She had imagined him kissing her, undressing her, and now, as Aksel unzipped her skirt and it fluttered to the floor, Mina allowed herself to sink deeper into the dream.

'Sweet Juliet,' he murmured as he bent his head and closed his lips around the tight bud of her nipple. The sensation was so exquisite that she cried out and arched her body like a slender bow, offering him her breasts and gasping with pleasure when he suckled her nipples in turn until they were swollen and tender.

She wanted to touch him as he was touching her and tore open his shirt buttons, parting the edges of his black silk shirt to reveal his golden tanned body. His skin gleamed like satin stretched taut over the defined ridges of his abdominal muscles. Dark blond hairs covered his chest and arrowed down over his flat stomach. Mina traced the fuzzy path with her fingers, but hesitated when she reached the waistband of his trousers as a voice of caution inside her head reminded her that her last sexual experience had been three years ago with a boyfriend she had dated for over a year.

Her heart-rate slowed and thudded painfully beneath her ribs. She must be crazy to think of having sex with a stranger. Aksel had proved that she could trust him when he had rescued her from the youths in the alleyway, and she was certain that if she called a halt now he would accept her decision. The sensible thing to do would be to tell him that she had changed her mind, but as she stared at his sculpted face with its slashing cheekbones and sensual mouth she could not formulate the words. The fire in his ice-blue eyes melted her resolve to walk away from him, and desire pooled hotly between her thighs when he stroked the bare strip of skin above the lace band of her hold-up stockings.

He held her gaze as he eased her panties aside and ran a finger up and down her moist opening until he felt her relax, allowing him to gently part her and slide deep into her silken heat.

'Beautiful,' he murmured when he discovered how aroused she was. He kissed her again with a blatant sensuality that drugged her senses so that she was barely aware of him removing the rest of her underwear before stripping out of his own clothes. He moved away from her for a moment, and she drew a shaky breath as she watched him take a protective sheath from the bedside drawer and slide it over his erection.

'I'm sure you agree that we don't want to take any risks,' he murmured.

Mina nodded mutely, shocked to realise that she was so caught up in the heat of sexual excitement she had not given a thought to contraception. Luckily Aksel was thinking clearly, but the fact that he was prepared for sex emphasised that his level of experience was far greater than hers. Doubt crept into her mind and she hoped he would not find her disappointing.

Her thoughts were distracted as he drew her into his arms once more. His powerful, muscular body reminded Mina of a golden-haired Norse god, but although he looked as formidable as a Viking warrior his hands were gentle as he cupped her bottom and lifted her against him.

She caught her breath when she felt the solid length of his erection jab into her belly.

'Wrap your legs around me,' he bade her tautly.

Trembling with anticipation, she gripped his shoulders for support and locked her ankles behind his back. Carefully he guided his thick shaft between her thighs and Mina buried her face against his neck to muffle her soft moan as he possessed her with a devastating powerful thrust. Her internal muscles stretched as he filled her. He withdrew slowly and then drove into her again, each thrust harder than the last so that her excitement swiftly mounted to fever pitch.

His shoulder muscles rippled beneath her hands as he supported her, making her aware of his immense strength. The sensation of him moving inside her was amazing, incredible, and indescribably beautiful. The world was spinning faster and faster, drawing her into a vortex of pleasure that grew more intense as he increased his pace. It was all happening too quickly. She gasped, feeling overwhelmed by Aksel's urgent passion and her equally urgent response to him.

'Angel, I'm sorry, I can't wait,' he groaned. He tightened his grip on her bottom and thrust so deeply into her that Mina wondered how much more she could take before her body shattered. She looked into his brilliant blue eyes and saw her need reflected in his burning gaze. His expression was almost tortured and she sensed he was fighting for control. He tipped his head back so that the veins on his neck stood out, and at the moment he exploded inside her Mina felt the first powerful ripples of her orgasm radiate out from her central core, and she gave a keening cry as she fell with him into ecstasy.

It was a long time before the world settled back on its axis, but eventually reality returned, bringing with it a tidal wave of guilt.

'I…I should go,' Mina whispered. She could taste tears at the back of her throat and forced herself to swallow them. There would be time for recriminations later, but her immediate aim was to slide off the bed where Aksel had laid her a few moments ago, and get dressed with as much dignity as possible—given the circumstances.

She stifled the urge to laugh hysterically as she considered the circumstances. It wasn't every night that she had wild and abandoned sex with a stranger—or any kind of sex, for that matter. A little moan of pain and shame rose in her throat and she bit down hard on her lip as she forced herself to look at the blond Viking sprawled beside her. Now that they were lying down she could admire the full glory of his naked body, the long legs and lean hips, the powerful abdominal muscles and broad chest.

Her eyes jerked to the one area of his body that she had avoided looking at. Even half aroused he was—

magnificent. Her stomach squirmed as she remembered how big he had felt when he had slowly filled her. Oh, God, what had she been thinking? Pretty much the same thoughts that were in her head now, Mina acknowledged with a choked sound of self-disgust.

She sat up and told herself it was ridiculous to feel shy that he was looking at her bare breasts when—let's face it—he'd done a lot more than simply look.

'Hey—angel?' Aksel propped himself up on one elbow and frowned when Mina quickly turned away from him. His gut clenched as he glimpsed a betraying shimmer in her eyes. *She was crying!* The idea that he had caused her to cry filled him with guilt. He had acted like a barbarian, he thought disgustedly. It was no excuse that for the first time in his life his iron self-restraint had been breached by her achingly sweet response to him. 'What's wrong?' he asked softly. 'Where are you going?'

Were there rules for this sort of occasion? If so, Mina did not know the rules. 'I thought I'd go home…now that…now that we've…' She watched his frown deepen and hoped he wasn't going to suggest they had dinner. The idea of sitting in that plush dining room while they were served by waiters who could probably guess what they'd had for an appetiser sent a shudder through her.

She tensed as he cupped her jaw and tilted her face to him.

'I didn't mean to make you cry, angel,' he said roughly. 'I'm sorry—I was too fast—too impatient…'

'*No*—' Mina did not want him to take the blame. He had nothing to blame himself for. 'It's not your fault—it's mine. It's just that I've never in my life gone to bed with a complete stranger…' her voice wobbled '…and I'm embarrassed.'

He did not seem to have listened to her, and doubt and remorse darkened his eyes. 'Angel...I should have—'

She shook her head, desperate to reassure him. 'You did everything right. It was...perfect.' She swallowed, thinking of those moments when she had come apart in his arms. Nothing had prepared her for the physical or emotional intensity of her orgasm. She had connected with him on a deeply fundamental level—as if they were each two halves of a whole—and even now she could not forget that feeling. 'It was beautiful,' she said huskily.

'For me too.' Aksel was surprised to find it was the truth. He leaned forwards and brushed his mouth over hers, felt the soft tremble of her lips and gently pulled her down so her head lay on his chest, and he stroked her hair. She reminded him of a young colt, nervous and unsure, ready to run away at any moment. Certainly she was not like the sophisticated women who occasionally shared his bed. Not at the palace, of course. Royal protocol demanded that only his wife could sleep with him in the prince's bedchamber. But he owned a private house a few kilometres out of Storvhal's capital city, Jonja, where he took his lovers, and also a cabin in the mountains where he took no one.

Making love with Mina had been unlike anything he'd ever experienced with other women. But he had known it would be. He'd known when he'd watched Juliet on stage and had been captivated by her sweet innocence mixed with exquisite sensuality that she would fulfil all his fantasies.

'I'm glad it was as good for you as it was for me,' he murmured. He rolled over, pinning her beneath him, and smiled when he heard her indrawn breath as he pushed his swelling, hardening shaft between her unresisting thighs. 'Something so good should be repeated, do you agree, angel?'

* * *

Life, Aksel mused, had a habit of throwing up problems when you least expected them. He rolled onto his side and studied his current problem. Mina's long auburn hair streamed across the pillows like a river of silk and her dark eyelashes lay on her cheeks in stark contrast to her creamy complexion. The sunlight filtering through the blinds revealed a sprinkling of tiny golden freckles on her nose. She looked curiously innocent and yet incredibly sexy as she moved and the sheet slipped down to expose one milky-pale breast tipped with a rose-pink nipple.

Aksel felt himself harden and he almost gave in to the delicious throb of desire that flooded through him. Only the realisation that if it was light outside then it could not be very early forced him to abandon the idea of drawing Mina into his arms. The clock showed that it was seven a.m. His private jet was scheduled to fly him and the members of the trade delegation back to Storvhal at eight-thirty, and he had a series of meetings booked for the afternoon before he was due to host a dinner party at the palace this evening.

Cursing beneath his breath, he sprang out of bed before he succumbed to the temptation of Mina's delectable body. Striding into the en-suite bathroom, he acknowledged that he had thrown his personal rule book out of the window when he had spent the night with her at his hotel. She was hardly the first woman he'd had sex with. He was thirty-five and did not live the life of a monk. But he chose his lovers from the tight-knit group of Storvhal's aristocracy. The women he met socially understood the need for discretion and ensured that details of the prince's private affairs never came to the attention of the media.

Falling asleep with Mina in his arms in a haze of sated exhaustion had compounded his folly, Aksel thought ruefully as he stood beneath an ice-cold shower. Meeting her had thrown up all kinds of problems, starting with the fact that she did not know who he was. Maybe that was why making love with her had been so amazing. Last night he had been able to forget for a few hours that he was a prince. He had just been a man blown away by his desire for a beautiful young woman who had captivated him since he had seen her in the role of Juliet.

But now the fantasy was over and he must focus on his royal duties. Frowning, Aksel reached for a towel embroidered with the monogram of the hotel. He knew he should feel grateful that he lived a life of great privilege, but he had learned during the twelve years that he had been monarch that personal freedom was the greatest privilege of all, and this morning more than at any other time in his life he was acutely aware that it was a luxury denied to him.

Mina breathed a sigh of relief as she peeped from beneath her lashes and watched Aksel walk into the bathroom. The sight of his broad back and taut buttocks evoked a melting sensation in the pit of her stomach. It was not only his golden hair and skin that reminded her of a Norse god. Last night he had demonstrated his formidable strength and energy—not to mention inventiveness, she thought, flushing hotly as memories of the various ways he had made love to her crowded her mind.

When she'd woken a few minutes ago and felt his erection nudge her thigh, her pulse had quickened with anticipation. But she'd pretended to be asleep when she had realised that the batteries in her hearing aids had died.

She had no idea how he would react if she revealed that she was partially deaf. They might have enjoyed a night of wild and totally amazing sex, but Aksel was still a stranger she had met in a pub, and in the cold light of day Mina felt a growing sense of shame at her wantonness. Her behaviour had been completely out of character, but Aksel did not know that.

She did not have a clue what the protocol was when you woke up in a man's hotel bedroom. What was she supposed to say to him? Thanks very much for the best sex I've ever had? She bit her lip. Okay, she'd behaved like an idiot and she felt vulnerable and out of her depth. It was imperative that she took control of the situation, and her first priority was to change the batteries in her hearing aids.

Conscious that Aksel might emerge from the bathroom at any moment, Mina did not waste time collecting up her clothes that were scattered across the floor, and instead wrapped a silk sheet from the bed around her before going to look for her handbag. Last night she had been too engrossed in Aksel to take much notice of her surroundings, but now she realised that this must be the hotel's penthouse suite. The door from the bedroom led into a luxurious sitting room, and beyond that was the dining room.

Her bare feet sank into the thick-pile carpet. She could only guess how much it would cost to stay in the lavish suite, and she wondered exactly what job Aksel did for his government.

In the dining room, the curtains had been opened and the table was set out for breakfast. The aroma of coffee and freshly baked rolls was enticing and Mina realised she was starving. Her handbag was on the chair where she had left it, and luckily the spare batteries she always carried with her were charged. It took a couple of seconds to replace the batteries in her hearing aids. She felt less vulnerable when she could hear again and her urgency to sneak out of Aksel's suite was replaced with a more acute need to allay her hunger pangs.

She was halfway through eating a roll spread with honey when she sensed that she was no longer alone. Glancing over her shoulder, she saw Aksel watching her from the doorway.

'You look like you're enjoying that,' he murmured.

It was ridiculous to feel embarrassed, Mina told herself. But she was conscious that she was naked beneath the sheet and that her nipples—still swollen from Aksel's ministrations last night—were clearly visible jutting beneath the silk. Colour flared on her cheeks as she remembered how he had kissed every inch of her body and suckled her breasts before he'd moved lower and pushed her legs apart to bestow the most intimate kiss of all.

Her appetite disappeared and she put the roll down on a plate. 'I hope you don't mind. I was hungry.'

'I'm not surprised,' he drawled, his eyes glinting. 'I ordered breakfast for you. After all, it's my fault you missed dinner last night.'

He couldn't take all the blame. It wasn't as if he'd forced her to stay with him, Mina thought guiltily. Her heart thudded as he walked towards her. Last night he had looked like a rock star in his leather jacket, but this morning he was dressed in a superbly tailored grey suit, white silk shirt and an ice-blue tie that matched the colour of his eyes. He was a suave and sophisticated stranger, and Mina clutched the sheet tighter round her. 'I should get dressed,' she mumbled.

'I wish you could stay as you are.' His voice thickened as he cupped her bare shoulders and pulled her towards him. 'Making love to you last night was amazing, and I wish the night could have lasted for ever.'

Mina's heart leapt as he dipped his head and kissed

her. She'd had no idea how Aksel would react after their night of passion, and had mentally prepared for him to state that it had been a mistake. The tenderness in his kiss was unexpected and utterly beguiling. She closed her eyes and melted against him, and the world disappeared as she was swept away by his sensual mastery.

It was a long time before he lifted his mouth from hers. 'You taste of honey,' he said huskily. With obvious reluctance he dropped his hands from her. 'My car is waiting to take me to the airport, but of course I'll take you home first.'

Her heart plummeted as his words catapulted her back to reality. 'You're flying back to Storvhal today, aren't you?'

'I have to, I'm afraid.' Aksel glanced at his watch and his jaw clenched. There was no time now to explain to Mina who he was. He could never escape the responsibilities that came with being a ruling monarch, but he was unwilling to accept that he would never see her again. However, inviting her to Storvhal would be fraught with difficulties.

'What about you? Do you have any plans now that the production of *Romeo and Juliet* has finished its run at the Globe?'

Perhaps later today she would hear if the play was going to Broadway, but Mina saw no point in mentioning it, or that she had an interview arranged for a position as a drama therapist with a health-care trust. She was by no means certain to get the job, and even if she were to be offered it there was still the problem of telling her father that she wanted to pull out of the play.

She shrugged. 'I don't have anything planned for the next couple of weeks. In the acting profession it's known as resting,' she said drily.

'I have to go to Paris at the end of next week. I was thinking about staying on for a couple of days to do some sightseeing.' Aksel paused and looked deeply into Mina's eyes. 'Would you like to meet up and spend the week-end with me?'

He wanted to meet her in Paris—the city of lovers! She strove to sound cool, despite the fact that her heart was racing because he wanted to see her again. 'That could be fun.'

A flame flickered in his blue eyes. 'I can guarantee it.' Unable to resist the lure of her soft mouth, Aksel bent his head, but at that moment his phone rang and he stifled a frustrated sigh when he saw that the call was from his PA. 'Excuse me, I need to take this,' he murmured.

Mina hurried back to the master bedroom. The tangled sheets on the bed were an embarrassing reminder of the passionate night she had spent with Aksel, but she felt better for knowing that it hadn't been a one-night stand. In the en-suite bathroom she bundled her hair into a shower cap and took a quick shower. It would be a mistake to read too much into his invitation to Paris, but the fact that he wanted to spend a weekend with her surely meant that he wanted to get to know her better—and not only in the bedroom.

A lifetime of practice allowed Aksel to greet Mina with an easy smile that disguised his tense mood when she walked back into the room. Her skirt looked even more crumpled after it had spent the night screwed up on the floor, and her long auburn hair fell in silky disarray around her shoulders, but her rather bohemian style was not foremost in his mind as he ushered her into the lift.

'The car is waiting round the back of the hotel,' he told her. He wondered what his PA's terse message meant. 'A situation has arisen' could mean anything. He hoped to God the trade deal hadn't fallen through.

Leading Mina to the rear of the lobby, he opened the door through which they had entered the hotel the previous night. A gust of wind whipped up the steps and lifted the hem of her skirt to reveal her slim thighs and lace stocking tops.

'*Oh…*' She frantically tried to push the lightweight material down. Another gust of wind almost knocked her off her feet and Aksel slid his arm around her waist to clamp her to his side as they walked out of the hotel.

'*Mina—over here!*' a voice called, and a flashbulb flared in the grey street. As Aksel turned his head towards the light the voice called again, '*Prince Aksel—fantastic!* Mina—you're a star. I asked you to give me a scoop, and this is gonna hit the headlines and make me rich!'

'What the hell…?' Cursing, Aksel glanced down at Mina's white face before shooting a furious glare at the man standing on the opposite pavement, holding a long-lens camera.

'Sir…' The chauffeur drew the car up against the kerb and jumped out, but the rear door had already been opened from inside by Aksel's PA.

'Quickly, sir…'

Aksel hardly needed to be told. He bundled Mina into the car before sliding in next to her, and the chauffeur slammed the door. As the car pulled away Aksel ran a hand through his hair and glared at the bespectacled young man sitting opposite him. 'Would you like to tell me what in hell's name is going on, Ben?'

CHAPTER FOUR

AKSEL'S PA, BENEDICT LINDBURG, grimaced. 'The paparazzi are swarming at the front of the hotel. I hoped you would be able to leave through the back door without being spotted.'

Glancing over his shoulder, Aksel could still see the florid-faced press photographer focusing his camera on the back of the car. 'I recognise him,' he said slowly. He looked at Mina, who was huddled into her jacket. 'That man came into the pub last night, and you looked at him as though you knew him.' His eyes narrowed on the twin spots of colour that flared on her white face. 'You told me he was no one in particular.'

He frowned as a curious, almost hunted expression flitted across Mina's face. 'Angel, who was that man? Do you have a problem?'

'With respect, sir, *you* have a problem,' Benedict Lindburg said quietly, handing Aksel a newspaper.

It took him a matter of seconds to skim the front page and he cursed savagely. 'What are the chances of us keeping this story contained?' he asked his PA.

'None,' was the short reply. 'The photo of you and Miss Hart entering the hotel through a back door last night has already been picked up by the media in Storvhal and is headline news. The pictures taken a few moments ago will doubtless already be posted on social media sites.'

Aksel's jaw clenched. 'Damn the paparazzi to hell.'

'I don't understand,' Mina said shakily. She had been shocked into silence when she had seen the journalist Steve Garratt as she and Aksel had emerged from the hotel, but she was puzzled by Aksel's reaction. 'What story? Why does it matter if we were seen going into the hotel last night?'

She recalled her suspicion that Aksel had an important role working for his country's government. Steve Garratt's words pushed into her head. The journalist had called out *Prince Aksel*. She stared at the newspaper photo of her and Aksel entering the hotel with their arms around each other. Above the picture the headline proclaimed *The Prince and the Showgirl!*

Mina turned stunned eyes on Aksel's hard-boned profile, trying frantically to recall any information she had read about Storvhal. The country was a principality—rather like Monaco was—an independent state with close connections to Norway, ruled by a monarch.

Realisation hit her like an ice-cold shower. 'You're a *prince*?' she choked.

'Prince Aksel the Second is head of the Royal House of Thoresen and Supreme Ruler of Storvhal,' the young man with the glasses said in a clipped tone. His expression behind his lenses was disapproving as he studied Mina's crumpled clothes.

She flushed, and asked tightly, 'And you are?'

'Benedict Lindburg, His Highness's personal assistant.'

His Highness! Mina bit her lip and stared at Aksel, wondering if she would wake up in a minute. If last night had seemed unreal, the events unfolding this morning were unbelievable. 'Why didn't you tell me?'

He gave her an odd, intent look. 'So you maintain that you did not know my identity when we met in the pub?'

'Of course I didn't.' Her voice faltered as she watched a muscle flicker in his jaw. There was no hint of his sexy, crooked smile on his mouth. His lips were set in a stern line and his face looked as though it had been sculpted from marble. 'Aksel…' she said uncertainly.

'Someone must have tipped off the press last night and told them that we would be entering the hotel through the back door.'

Aksel's voice was expressionless but inside his head his thoughts ran riot. Nothing made sense. No one had known that he had invited Mina to his hotel—except for Mina herself, his brain pointed out. He tensed as his mind violently rejected the possibility that he had made the most spectacular misjudgement of his life. But a memory slid like a snake into his mind and spewed poison.

'You sent a text message to someone as the taxi drew up outside the hotel,' he reminded her.

Mina's eyes flashed at his accusatory tone. 'I sent a message to my friend Kat to confirm that I would be at a cast meeting at the theatre this morning. I'll show you the damn text if you don't believe me,' she said hotly. Her eyes met Aksel's and she felt chilled by the cold speculation in his gaze.

His PA broke the tense silence. 'Is the meeting to discuss the announcement made in the press this morning that the Joshua Hart Theatre company will be performing *Romeo and Juliet* on Broadway?'

Mina blinked. 'There's been an announcement? I haven't spoken to my father but I have heard he has been in negotiations to take the play to New York.'

'The news about the play has received extra prominence in the media, due no doubt to speculation about your relationship with Prince Aksel,' Benedict Lindburg said stiffly.

Aksel swore beneath his breath. Since he had become ruler of Storvhal he had never lowered his guard, never slipped up—until he had looked into a pair of deep green eyes and lost his head. Shame seared him. Perhaps he was as weak as his father after all. If he was labelled a playboy prince by the press in Storvhal it could cause irreparable damage to his reputation and even to the monarchy.

He stared at Mina and despised himself for wanting to kiss her tremulous mouth. 'The journalist who was waiting for us this morning—he knew your name, and he said he'd asked you to give him a scoop,' Aksel said grimly. 'He *was* the same man who was in the pub.' He recalled the strange expression on Mina's face when she had seen the man the previous evening, and the truth hit him like a blow to his stomach. 'The journalist is a friend of yours, and you tipped him off that I'd invited you to my hotel last night.'

'I didn't!'

Her beautiful eyes widened. A man could drown in those deep green pools, Aksel thought. Hell, he could feel himself floundering, wanting to believe the shocked outrage in her voice. Only a gifted actress could feign such innocence. Mina had played Juliet so convincingly, taunted a voice in Aksel's head. She made a living out of pretence and playing make-believe.

Rage burned inside him, but beneath his anger was a savage feeling of betrayal that despite her denial Mina *must* have spoken to the press. He was aware of the same hollow sensation in his gut that he had felt as a young man, when he had learned that his mother had betrayed him.

When Aksel had found out that Karena did not really love him, he had been hurt. But far worse had been the discovery that his mother had encouraged the Russian model to seduce him, promising her a life of fame, fortune and luxury. After Prince Geir's death, Irina had had strong financial reasons for wanting to maintain a link between Russia and Storvhal, and she had believed it would be beneficial for her if her son married a Russian woman. But when her plan had been revealed, Aksel had realised just how cold and calculating his mother was, and how little she cared about him.

Helvete! If his own mother could betray him, why was he surprised that a woman he had picked up in a bar had done the same? he derided himself. Bitter experience had taught him never to trust any woman and he was furious with himself for being taken in by Mina's air of innocence.

Mina could tell from Aksel's cold expression that he did not believe her. 'I *didn't* know you are a prince,' she repeated. 'Even if I had, why would I have tipped off a journalist?'

'To create publicity for your father's theatre company,' Benedict Lindburg suggested smoothly.

'Keep out of this.' Mina rounded on the PA fiercely. 'You don't know anything about me.'

'As a matter of fact I know everything about you.' The PA handed a folder to Aksel with an apologetic shrug. 'The photo of you and Miss Hart was posted on social media sites shortly after it was taken last night. As soon as I was alerted to it I ran a security check on Miss Hart. My report includes details of Miss Hart's acting career in England and also in the United States.'

The colour drained from Mina's face as she stared at the folder in Aksel's hand. Without doubt his PA had unearthed the story about her relationship—her alleged white-hot affair—with the film director Dexter Price, which some of the media had labelled a publicity stunt to promote the film she had starred in. She had done nothing wrong, Mina reminded herself. She had not deserved to be vilified by the press, but what chance was there of Aksel believing her side of the story when she looked as guilty as hell of tipping off the journalist Steve Garratt.

She looked into Aksel's eyes and felt chilled to the bone. The Viking lover with the sexy smile had turned into a stranger. He had always been a stranger, she reminded herself. Just because he had made love to her as though she were the most precious person on the planet did not prove anything other than that he was very good at sex.

Shame swept through her as she remembered how she had responded to him in bed. She did not know what had come over her. And him a *prince*! She froze when Aksel opened the folder and sought his gaze, her eyes unconsciously pleading. If only they could go back to last night, to the private, magical world they had created.

'Aksel…' she whispered.

For a heartbeat she thought he was going to listen to her. Something flared in his eyes, and he stared at her mouth as if he wanted to kiss her. But then his jaw hardened and he deliberately turned away and looked down at the open file.

Mina could not bear to sit beside him while he read about the most humiliating episode in her life. The traffic was crawling around Marble Arch, and the car came to a standstill. The only thought in Mina's head was to run from Aksel—something she should have done last night, she acknowledged grimly. She must have been out of her mind to have slept with a stranger.

Before he realised her intention she opened the car door and scrambled out into the midst of four lanes of traffic.

Aksel sprang forwards and tried to grab hold of her. 'Don't be an idiot!' he yelled. 'You'll be killed!' His heart was in his mouth as he watched her weave through the cars, taxis and buses. Moments later he glimpsed Mina's long auburn hair as she disappeared down the steps leading to the underground station. Slowly he sank back in his seat, fighting a fierce urge to chase after her.

Benedict pulled the car door shut. The PA was startled when he thought he glimpsed emotion in the Prince of Storvhal's eyes. 'Sir...I'm sorry,' he said hesitantly.

The hot flood of rage inside Aksel had solidified into a cold, hard knot. It was bad enough that Mina had made a fool of him, and worse that his stupidity had been witnessed by a member of his staff.

His jaw tightened. He had certainly been a fool to have thought—even fleetingly—that making love with Mina had been somehow special. She'd had a few clever tricks—that was all. Like the way she had focused her big green eyes intently on his mouth. She'd made him feel as if he were the only man in the world for her.

He glanced at his PA and raised an eyebrow. 'I don't require your sympathy, Ben,' he drawled. 'I simply want you to get on with your job. Have you confirmed my meeting with the Danish Prime Minister yet?'

He must have been imagining things, Benedict told himself. The Ice Prince's face was as emotionless as always. Suitably chastened, the PA murmured, 'I'll do it right away, sir.'

* * *

Mina could hear her father's raised voice from the other end of the corridor.

'*Get out of my sight,*' Joshua Hart roared. 'I will not put up with guttersnipes from the tabloid press harassing me with tittle-tattle and nonsense.'

Forewarned that journalists must be in her father's office, Mina darted into a broom cupboard moments before two men clutching cameras and recording equipment shot past.

It was no surprise that the other members of the play's cast seemed to be keeping out of the director's way. Joshua in a temper reminded Mina of an angry bear, and she took a deep breath before she peeped cautiously around his office door.

'Oh, it's you.' He greeted her with a scowl. 'I hope you haven't brought any more damn journalists with you.'

'No.' Mina was pretty sure she had managed to slip through a side door of the Globe without being seen by the journalists milling about outside the theatre. She gave him a hesitant smile. 'It's great news about the play going to New York.'

Her father snorted. 'I tried to phone you last night to tell you the news first, before I announced it to the rest of the cast, but you didn't answer. I suppose you were with this chap of yours.' He glared at Mina from beneath his bushy eyebrows. 'It's all over the papers that you are dating a prince.'

Mina's heart sank when she saw copies of several of the morning's newspapers on her father's desk. The photograph on the front page showed her and Aksel entering his hotel through a back door, and it was clear from their body language that they had been on their way to bed.

'I'm not dating him,' she said quickly, but her father did not appear to have heard her.

'I would have thought you'd had enough publicity when you got involved with that film director in America. Heaven knows, you're an adult and you can lead your life how you want,' Joshua exploded. 'But having your love-life plastered across the newspapers is not the sort of publicity I want for the Hart family or my theatre company. Have you thought that this could have a detrimental effect when the play opens on Broadway?'

According to Dexter Price there was no such thing as bad publicity, Mina thought darkly. 'In what way do you mean detrimental?' she asked her father.

'We're performing Shakespeare on Broadway,' Joshua snapped. 'I don't want the production to turn into a soap opera because Juliet is sleeping with a European aristocrat. You know how fascinated the Americans are by that sort of thing.'

Mina bit her lip as she stared at her father's furious face. She had hoped for his support but she should have known that he would be more concerned about the play than her. Joshua had been an unpredictable parent while she was growing up, and Mina and her brother and sisters had learned to deal with his mood swings and artistic temperament.

'I assure you I didn't ask for the publicity,' she said stiffly. 'I won't be seeing Aks...the prince...again so you need not worry that I'll attract adverse press coverage.'

It was obvious from the way Aksel had been so quick to believe the worst of her that he'd never had any intention of meeting her in Paris. He was a prince, for heaven's sake, and she had been a one-night stand. She swallowed the sudden lump in her throat, remembering how he had kissed her with such beguiling tenderness at the hotel that morning. He had made her think that he genuinely did want to see her again. She grimaced. His performance had been worthy of an award for best actor.

'Your mother's worried about you,' Joshua muttered. 'You'd better phone her.' He sat down at his desk. 'I've told the cast to assemble on the stage and I'll be along to discuss the New York project when I've made a couple of calls.'

Kat Nichols was the first person Mina saw when she walked through the theatre.

'Mina! I couldn't believe it when I saw the newspapers. Who would have guessed that the blond hunk from the pub is a *prince*?'

Not me, unfortunately, Mina thought ruefully.

Kat looked at her closely. 'Are you okay? Some of the papers have dragged up a story about you and a film director in LA.' She could not hide her curiosity. 'What did exactly happen between you and Dexter Price?'

Mina bit her lip. Now that the newspapers had reprinted the lies about her, she might as well tell Kat the truth.

'I'd been picked for a lead role in what was touted as the next big blockbuster film,' she said heavily. 'During filming I formed a close relationship with Dexter. I naïvely believed that he wanted to keep our friendship quiet to protect me from gossip. He never took me to popular bars or restaurants where we might be seen together. But a journalist got wind that something was going on and managed to take some damning photos of us.'

She grimaced. 'I only ever kissed Dex, but pictures of us were splashed across the newspapers and appeared to prove that we were having a sordid affair. It turned out that Dex was married—although he had told me he was divorced. Not only that, but his wife had been diagnosed with breast cancer.'

'Oh, God, how awful for her, and for you,' Kat murmured.

'The press labelled me a heartless marriage-wrecker,' Mina said flatly as she relived the nightmare that had unfolded in LA. 'Dex lied to me. I hadn't known he had a wife, let alone that she was seriously ill. I felt so guilty that she had been hurt, but Dex didn't care. He actually said that the publicity about our relationship would be good for the film.'

'What a bastard,' Kat said fiercely.

'I wanted to come home straight away, but I had to finish the film. Too many people would have been affected if I'd pulled out. Luckily there were only two more weeks of filming left but I was hounded by the paparazzi until I left LA.'

'Some journalists have been at the theatre this morning, trying to get members of the cast to talk about you. But no one has,' Kat added quickly.

'No one knows much about me,' Mina said drily. Although she got on well with most of the other cast members, she guarded her privacy. She felt sick knowing that everyone would be gossiping about her personal life, and her temper simmered because once again she had unwittingly become headline news. If Aksel had told her that he was the Prince of Storvhal she would never have agreed to go to his hotel. Her bitter experience with Dex had taught her to steer clear of people who were in the public eye.

She went with Kat to join the other actors, who were gathered on the stage. The buzz of conversation faded and there was an awkward silence until Laurence Adams, who played Mercutio, said brightly, 'That was a great

PR stunt, Mina. The story about your relationship with a prince who is supposedly one of Europe's most eligible bachelors has gone global on the same day that it was announced that our production of *Romeo and Juliet* is going to Broadway. With all the media interest I reckon we'll be a sell-out in New York.'

No way, Mina silently vowed, would she allow any of the cast to know how humiliated she felt. When she had been growing up, being the only deaf child in a mainstream school had taught Mina to develop a tough shell and hide her feelings of insecurity and hurt when she was teased for being 'different'. Acting had become a means of survival, and now she utilised all her theatrical skills to brazen out the embarrassing situation.

Lifting her chin, she said airily, 'Yeah, I'm thrilled that I was pictured with a prince. Apparently the story is on all the American news networks and everyone in New York will know that the play will be opening there soon. I'm sure you're right and we'll perform to a full house every night.'

Several of the cast cheered, but beside her Kat stiffened and muttered warningly, 'Mina—he's here!'

Mina's heart missed a beat. She turned her head to tell Kat that she did not find the joke funny, but the words froze on her lips as she looked up at the gallery and saw a golden-haired Viking staring down at the stage.

Aksel's stern face could have been carved from granite, and even from a distance Mina felt chilled by his icy stare. He did not say a word, but as she replayed her statement in her head, her frustration boiled over.

'I…I didn't mean what I said,' she called up to him.

His silence was crushing. He stared at her for a few more seconds before he swung round and the sound of his footsteps as he strode from the gallery reverberated around the theatre.

'I swear, I didn't know you are a damn prince,' Mina shouted after him. But he did not turn his head and moments later he had disappeared.

He had walked out without giving her a chance to explain! Who was this cold man who had replaced her caring lover of the night before? The fiasco of the damning photograph in the newspaper was *his* fault. His royal status made him a target for the paparazzi. Her stomach lurched as she realised that Steve Garratt must have recognised Aksel in the pub the previous evening. The journalist must have seen her get into the taxi with Aksel and followed them to the hotel. Garratt had certainly got the scoop he'd wanted, she thought bitterly.

She choked back an angry sob. Aksel had refused to listen to her—just as her father so often did not listen. When she had first lost her hearing, Mina had also lost her confidence to speak. Years of speech therapy had helped her to find her voice again, and thanks to her hearing aids she was able to disguise her hearing impairment. But deep inside her there still lingered the insecure little girl who had felt trapped and alone in a silent world. Being deprived of one of her senses made her feel invisible and insignificant.

Damn Aksel for ignoring her, she thought furiously as she ran through the theatre. She would make him listen to her!

But when she reached the exit there was no sign of him and the only people outside the theatre were some journalists. The sound of a car's engine drew her attention to the road, and her heart sank when she saw the sleek black limousine that had collected her and Aksel from the hotel earlier pull away from the kerb.

The journalists spotted her and crowded around the door. 'Miss Hart—are you in a relationship with Prince Aksel of Storvhal?'

'Are you hoping that the prince will visit you while you are performing in New York?'

Kat rushed up as Mina slammed the door shut to block out the journalists' questions.

'Joshua is in a furious temper,' Kat told her breathlessly. 'He's demanding to know why you invited the prince here to the theatre.'

Mina groaned. She could not cope with her father when he was in one of his unreasonable moods. But in fairness she could understand why he was angry with her. The announcement that he would be directing his theatre company's production of *Romeo and Juliet* on Broadway should have been a highlight of Joshua's career, but Mina had unwittingly stolen his thunder. The press were more interested in her relationship with a prince than in the play.

'I have to get away from here,' she muttered.

'My car is parked round the back. We might be able to slip out without being seen. But, Mina...' Kat hesitated, looking concerned. 'I drove past your flat on my way here this morning and saw press photographers outside.'

'I'm not going home,' Mina said grimly. 'Will you give me a lift to the airport?'

Benedict Lindburg, sitting in the front of the limousine with the driver, took one look at Aksel's face as he climbed into the rear of the car and wisely did not say a word.

At least his PA knew when to keep his opinion to himself, Aksel thought darkly as he hit a button to activate the privacy screen that separated him from the occupants in the front of the car. It was unlikely that his chief advisor would show the same diplomacy. He grimaced as his phone rang and Harald Petersen's name flashed on the caller display.

'It's a personal matter,' Aksel explained curtly, in answer to his advisor's query about why the royal flight from London to Storvhal had been delayed.

There was a tiny hesitation before Harald said smoothly, 'I understand that you have cancelled all your meetings for this afternoon. If you have a problem, sir, I hope that I can be of assistance.'

The problem—as Harald damn well knew—was the photograph and the headline *'The Prince and the Show-girl'* that had made the front page of the newspapers in England and Storvhal, and no doubt the rest of the world. But the real problem was *him*, Aksel thought grimly. He cursed the crazy impulse that had caused him to instruct his driver to turn the car around when they had been on the way to the airport, and take him to the Globe Theatre. But his conscience had been nagging. He had remembered the charity function that had been held at the Erskine hotel last night, and the members of the press who had been gathered outside to take pictures of the celebrity guests. It was possible that the paparazzi had been covering other entrances to the hotel, and Aksel had realised that he might have been wrong when he had accused Mina of tipping off a journalist that they would enter via a back door.

The article in the newspaper about her affair with a married film director in LA was damning, but when he'd read the sordid details Aksel had struggled to equate the heartless bimbo described in the paper with the woman who had responded with such sweet eagerness when he had made love to her. There had been a curious innocence to Mina that had touched something inside him. But now he knew it had been an act. Overhearing her at the theatre had ripped the blinkers from his eyes, and the realisation that she was as calculating and mercenary as his mother and Karena filled him with icy rage.

'The photograph in the newspapers of you and the English actress could have repercussions in Storvhal,' Harald Petersen murmured. 'I fear that people will be reminded of your father's playboy image, and it is imperative we think of a damage-limitation strategy. Perhaps you could issue a statement to deny that you are involved with Miss Hart—although that will be less believable now that there is a second photograph of you leaving the hotel with her.' Harald gave a pained sigh. 'I assume you will not be seeing her again. I'm afraid the Storvhalian people will not approve of you having an affair with her, and I am sure I do not need to remind you that your duty to your country must come before any other consideration.'

Aksel's jaw clenched and he tightened his grip on his phone until his knuckles whitened. 'You're right—you don't need to remind me of my duty,' he said harshly. '*Helvete!* You, above all people, Harald, know the sacrifice I made to ensure the stability of the country when Storvhal was on the brink of civil unrest. Only you, amongst my staff, know that Karena gave me an illegitimate child. My son is dead, and for eight years I have kept Finn's brief existence a secret because I understood that I must focus on ruling Storvhal and try to repair the damage my father caused to the monarchy.'

His tone became steely as he fought to disguise the rawness of his emotions. 'Do not throw duty in my face, Harald. I swore when I was crowned that I would fulfil the expectations that the people of Storvhal have of their prince, but I have paid a personal price that will haunt me for ever.'

Aksel ended the call and his head fell back against the leather car seat. He could feel his heart jerking painfully beneath his ribs as he replayed his conversation with his chief advisor in his mind. How *could* Harald have implied that he needed to be reminded of his duty to his country? He had given Storvhal everything. He had spent more than a decade paying for his father's sins, and had striven to be a perfect prince, even though it meant that he'd had to bury his grief for his son deep inside him.

The baby had been born in Russia and tragically had only lived for a few weeks. Losing Finn had ripped Aksel's heart out. Every time his grandmother spoke of the need for him to have an heir Aksel pictured his baby boy and felt a familiar ache in his chest. But his grandmother had no idea how he felt. No one in his life, apart from his chief advisor, knew about Finn.

His thoughts turned again to Mina and for some inexplicable reason the ache inside him intensified. His mouth twisted cynically. He'd had sex with her, but of course she had not touched him on an emotional level, he assured himself. Aksel had buried his heart with his baby son, and the Ice Prince—the name that he knew his staff called him behind his back—was incapable of feeling anything.

CHAPTER FIVE

NOTHING HAD PREPARED Mina for the bone-biting cold as she walked through the doors of Storvhal's international airport into a land of snow and ice.

'Are you sure you want to do this?' Kat had asked when she had dropped Mina off at Heathrow. 'Where on earth is Storvhal, anyway?'

'It's an island that stretches across the northern border of Norway and Russia.'

Kat had eyed Mina's thin cotton skirt and jacket doubtfully. 'Well, in that case you'd better borrow my coat.'

Mina had baulked at the idea of wearing her friend's purple leopard-print coat with a hood trimmed with pink marabou feathers but she hadn't had the heart to refuse. Now she was less concerned about Kat's eccentric taste in fashion, and was simply grateful that the eye-catching coat provided some protection against the freezing temperature, as did the fur-lined boots and gloves she had bought in the airport shop along with a few other essentials. But the coat and boots would not keep her warm for long when a sign on the airport wall displayed a temperature of minus six degrees.

The fact that it was dark at three o'clock in the afternoon was another shock. But she was in the Arctic Circle, Mina reminded herself. According to the tourist guide she had picked up, Storvhal would soon be in polar night—meaning that there would be no daylight at all from the end of October until February.

She did not plan to be in Storvhal for long—although admittedly her exact plans were sketchy. She had been furious with Aksel when she had flown from England, and determined to defend herself against his accusation that she had tipped off the journalist and was therefore responsible for the photograph of them in the papers. But now that she had arrived in his icy, alien country she was starting to question her sanity.

Her sister often teased her for being impulsive. Mina felt a sudden pang of longing to be in Sicily, at the castle Torre d'Aquila with Darcey and Salvatore. Her brother-in-law had made her feel so welcome when she had visited in the summer. It was wonderful that Darcey was so happy and in love. Mina could not help but feel a little envious that her sister was adored by her handsome husband. If she ever got married she hoped she would share a love as strong as theirs.

A blast of icy wind prompted Mina to walk towards a taxi parked outside the airport terminal. To her relief the driver spoke good English and he nodded when she asked him to take her to the royal palace, which was mentioned in the tourist guide.

'The palace is open to the public during the week. You should be in time for the last tour of the day,' he told her. 'It's very spectacular. It was built in the twelfth century by a Viking warrior who was the first prince of Storvhal. If you look at the newspaper,' the driver continued, 'you will see that our current prince has made the headlines today.'

Mina glanced at the newspaper on the seat beside her and her heart sank. The paper must be a later edition than the one she had seen earlier, and the photo on the front page was of her and Aksel emerging from the hotel that morning. The wind had whipped her skirt up to her thighs, and her tangled hair looked as if she had just got out of bed. Aksel had his arm around her and wore the satisfied expression of a man who had enjoyed a night of hot sex.

Oh, God! Mina cringed. The taxi driver glanced at her in his rear-view mirror and she was thankful that her face was hidden by the hood of her coat.

'According to the press reports, the prince is having an affair with an English actress. I feel sorry for him,' the driver continued. 'The people of Storvhal take great interest in Prince Aksel's private life. I guess they are afraid that he will turn out like his late father.'

'What was wrong with his father?' Mina was curious to learn any information about Aksel.

'Prince Geir was not a good monarch. People called him the playboy prince because he was more interested in partying with beautiful women on his yacht in Monaco than ruling the country.' The driver shrugged. 'It did not help his popularity when he married a Russian woman. Historically, Storvhalians have mistrusted Russia. Prince Geir was accused of making secret business deals with Russian companies and increasing his personal wealth by selling off Storvhal's natural resources.

'Since Prince Aksel has ruled Storvhal he has avoided any hint of scandal and has restored support for the monarchy,' the driver explained. 'He won't be pleased to have his personal life made public—and I'm sure the princess will be upset.'

Mina's heart lurched sickeningly. 'The *princess*…do you mean Prince Aksel is married?'

The memory of learning that Dexter had a wife and

was not divorced as he had told her was still raw in Mina's mind. Aksel had insisted that he was not married, but he could have lied. She shuddered to think that she might have been a gullible fool for a second time.

The driver did not appear to notice the sudden sharpness in her voice. 'Oh, no, I meant Princess Eldrun—Prince Aksel's grandmother. She ruled Storvhal with her husband, Prince Fredrik, for many years. When he died and Prince Geir inherited the throne the princess did not hide her disappointment that her son was a poor monarch. Geir was killed in a helicopter crash on his way to visit one of his many mistresses. It is common knowledge that Princess Eldrun hopes her grandson will choose a Storvhalian bride and provide an heir to the throne.'

They had been travelling along a main road, but now the taxi driver turned the car onto a gravel driveway that wound through a vast area of parkland. The frozen snow on the ground glittered in the bright glare of the street lamps, and the branches of the trees were spread like white lacy fingers against the night-dark sky. It was hard to believe that it was afternoon, Mina mused.

Her thoughts scattered as the royal palace came into view. With its white walls, tall turrets and arched windows, it looked like a fairy-tale castle, and the layer of powdery, glistening snow clinging to the roofs and spires reminded her of icing on top of a cake. The sight of guards in navy blue and gold uniforms standing in front of the palace gave her a jolt. For the first time it dawned on her that the man she had spent last night with, and who had made love to her with breathtaking passion, was actually a member of a royal dynasty.

The taxi driver dropped her at the public entrance to the palace and Mina joined the queue of people waiting to take a guided tour. An information leaflet explained that the public were allowed into the library and several reception rooms, which had been turned into a museum. The beautiful wood-panelled rooms filled with ancient tapestries and oil paintings were fascinating, but she was not in the mood for sightseeing.

She turned to the tour guide. 'Where can I see the prince?'

'You cannot see him—of course not.' The female guide looked shocked, but her expression lifted as she clearly thought that she had misunderstood. 'Do you mean you wish to buy a photograph of Prince Aksel? We sell souvenirs in the gift shop. The palace is about to close but you can visit the shop on your way out.'

The guide walked away, leaving Mina feeling a fool. Why had she thought that she would be able to stroll into the palace and bump into Storvhal's monarch? It was as likely as expecting to meet the Queen of England when Buckingham Palace was opened to the public in the summer. But the truth was she hadn't thought of anything past her urgency to find Aksel and convince him that she had not betrayed him to the press.

After learning from the taxi driver about Storvhal's royal family, and the unpopularity of Aksel's father, who had been known as the playboy prince, she could understand better why Aksel had reacted so angrily to the press allegations that they were having an affair.

The adrenaline that had been pumping through Mina's veins since she had arrived in Storvhal and mentally prepared herself for a showdown with Aksel drained away, and she felt exhausted—which was not surprising when she'd had very little sleep the previous night, she thought, flushing as erotic memories resurfaced. The knowledge that Aksel was somewhere in the vast palace but she could not meet him was bitterly frustrating.

She glanced out of the window and realised that she must be overlooking the grounds at the rear of the palace. A four-by-four was parked on the driveway and someone was about to climb into the driver's seat. The man was wearing a ski jacket; his hood slipped back, and Mina's heart missed a beat when she recognised the distinctive tiger stripes in his blond hair.

Aksel!

She tapped frantically on the window to gain his attention. He was going to drive away and there was nothing she could do to stop him! He did not look up, and she watched him take a mobile phone out of his jacket and walk back inside the palace.

Mina looked along the corridor and saw the guide shepherding the other people from the tour party into the gift shop. Walking as rapidly as she dared, she hurried past the shop and out of the palace before racing through the grounds. With every step she expected to be challenged by the palace guards, but no one seemed to have noticed her. When she reached the four-by-four she found the engine had been left running, but there was no sign of Aksel.

The freezing air made Mina's eyes sting, and she peered through the swirling snowflakes that had started to fall. She was likely to get frostbite if she stayed outside for much longer but she refused to give up her only opportunity to talk to Aksel. A few more minutes passed, and her toes and fingers became numb. There was nothing for it but to wait inside the vehicle, she decided as she opened the rear door and climbed inside.

The warmth of the interior of the four-by-four enveloped her. Gradually she stopped shivering, and as tiredness overwhelmed her she lay down on the seat and closed her eyes, promising herself that she would only rest them for a minute.

* * *

The snow was falling so thickly that the windscreen wipers could barely cope. Aksel knew that driving into the mountains in mid-October was a risk, but the weather reports had been clear, and he'd decided to visit the cabin for one last weekend before winter set in.

He guessed the blizzard had taken the forecasters by surprise. The road down in the valley was likely to be impassable already and there was no point turning round. Aksel was used to the harsh, fast-changing conditions of the Arctic landscape and wasn't worried that he would make it to the cabin, but he knew there was a chance he could be stranded there if the weather did not improve.

He probably should have listened to his chief advisor's plea to remain at the palace, he thought ruefully. But he had been in no mood to put up with Harald Petersen's pained expression as the chief advisor read the latest press revelations that Storvhal's ruling monarch was having a love affair with an English actress and apparently good-time girl, Mina Hart.

Love affair! Aksel gave a cynical laugh. Emotions had played no part in the night he had spent with Mina. If the press had accused him of having casual, meaningless sex with her it would have been closer to the truth. But he was meant to be above such behaviour, because, as Harald frequently reminded him, the population of Storvhal would not tolerate another playboy prince as his father had been.

Thank God he had managed to keep the story from his grandmother so far. Princess Eldrun's heart was weak and a rumour that her grandson might be following his father's reprobate lifestyle would be a devastating shock for her. Aksel's knuckles whitened on the steering wheel.

Mina's publicity stunt could have dire consequences for his grandmother's health.

A memory flashed into his mind of Mina's stricken face as he had walked away from her at the Globe Theatre earlier in the day. Damn it, he had overheard her admit that the rumours she was having an affair with him had earned her father's production of *Romeo and Juliet* extensive media coverage. So why did he still have a lingering doubt that he might have misjudged her?

Because he was a fool, that was why, he told himself angrily. He should despise Mina, but he could not stop thinking about her and remembering how she had felt in his arms, the softness of her skin when he had lowered his body onto hers. *Damn her*, he thought savagely, shifting position to try to ease the throb of his arousal.

A sudden movement in his rear-view mirror caught his attention. Something—a faceless figure—loomed up on the back seat of the four-by-four. Aksel's heart collided with his ribcage, and he swore, as shock and—hell, he wasn't ashamed to admit it—fear surged through him. His chief advisor's warnings that he should take more care of his personal safety jerked into his mind. But he refused to carry a weapon that had the potential to take a life. He had witnessed the utter finality of death when he had cradled his baby son's lifeless body in his arms. The experience had had a profound effect on him and made him appreciate the immeasurable value of life.

He only hoped that whoever had stowed away in his car valued *his* life. Most of the population of Storvhal supported his rule. However he could not ignore the fact that no leader or public figurehead was completely safe from the threat of assassination. *Was he going to feel a bullet in the back of his neck?*

The hell he was! His survival instinct kicked in and

he hit the brakes hard, causing the faceless figure to fall forwards. Adrenaline pumped through his veins as he leapt out of the truck and pulled open the rear door. The interior light automatically flicked on and Aksel stared in disbelief at the incongruous sight of a figure wearing a purple leopard-print coat with a hood trimmed with pink feathers.

'What in God's name…?' Conscious that the stowaway could have a weapon, Aksel grabbed hold of an arm, and with his other hand yanked the hood back to reveal a tumbling mass of silky auburn hair and a pair of deep green eyes.

'Mina?' His brain could not comprehend what his eyes were telling him. He was halfway up a glacier in the middle of a snowstorm and it was beyond belief that the woman who had haunted his thoughts all day was staring mutely at him.

'What are you doing? How did you get into my truck? *Hellvete!*' He lost his grip on his temper when she made no reply. The snow was swirling around him and he impatiently raked his damp hair off his brow and glared at her. 'What crazy game are you playing? Answer me, damn you. Why are you pretending to be deaf?'

'I'm not pretending.' At last she spoke in a tremulous voice that Aksel struggled to hear.

Mina stared at Aksel's furious face. She could tell he was shouting at her from the jerky way his lips moved, but she couldn't hear him. She could not hear anything. When she had woken, dazed and disorientated in the back of the four-by-four, it had taken her a few moments to work out why everything was silent. She had realised that her hearing-aid batteries had run down and remembered that she had fitted a new set at Aksel's hotel that morning, but the rechargeable batteries in her handbag had probably not been fully charged.

The faint gleam of the car's interior lamp cast shadows on Aksel's face and highlighted his sharp cheekbones and strong jaw. He was forbiddingly beautiful, and, despite the freezing wind whipping into the four-by-four, Mina felt a flood of warmth in the pit of her stomach.

She said shakily, 'I have a severe hearing impairment and rely on hearing aids to be able to hear.' She opened her hand and showed him the two tiny listening devices that she had removed from her ears. 'The batteries are dead, but I can lip-read if I watch your mouth when you speak.'

For one of only a handful of times in his life, Aksel had no idea what to say. 'Are you serious about being unable to hear, or are you playing some sort of sick joke?' he demanded.

'Of course I wouldn't joke about something like that,' Mina snapped. 'I've been deaf since I was a child. Most people don't know I can't hear because my hearing aids allow me to lead a normal life, and I'm good at hiding my disability from strangers,' she added with fierce pride.

'Last night we were as intimate as two people can get,' Aksel reminded her. 'I wouldn't call us strangers. Why didn't you tell me you are unable to hear?'

'I suppose for the same reason that you didn't tell me you are a prince.' Mina shrugged. 'I didn't feel ready to share personal confidences with you. And clearly we are still strangers, because otherwise you wouldn't have believed that I told the press about us.'

Aksel frowned. Snowdrifts were already forming around his legs, and more importantly around the wheels of the truck, and he knew he must keep the vehicle moving or risk becoming trapped on the exposed mountain road. But there were still a couple of questions he needed answered. 'Why the hell are you wearing a fancy-dress costume?'

Mina glanced ruefully at the horrendous purple coat. 'My friend lent me her coat because I only had a thin jacket. Kat has an…unusual fashion sense, but it was kind of her,' she said loyally.

'Do you mean to say that underneath that thing you're not wearing protective cold-weather clothing?'

'I didn't know I would need them when I got into your car at the palace. You had gone inside to talk on your phone and I decided to wait for you, but I fell asleep,' she explained when Aksel gave her a puzzled look.

That cleared up one mystery. 'I'm surprised you didn't bring your journalist friend with you,' he said bitterly.

'I'm not friendly with any journalists.'

'The man in the pub,' he reminded her.

She grimaced. 'I promise you Steve Garratt is no friend of mine.'

Aksel shook the snow out of his hair. He wished he could turn the truck around and drive Mina straight back to the airport, but the weather was worsening and his only option was to take her to the cabin.

'We'll have to save the rest of this discussion for later.' He turned away from her as he spoke. When she did not respond he realised that she had not heard him, and the only way they could communicate was for Mina to read his lips. Things were starting to fall into place—like the way she had focused intently on his face last night. He'd thought that she couldn't take her eyes off him because she found him attractive, but now he knew she had watched his lips when he spoke to disguise the fact that she was deaf.

She must have some guts to be so determined not

to allow her hearing impairment to affect her life, he thought, feeling a grudging admiration for her. He wondered if she felt vulnerable without her hearing aids. He couldn't imagine what it was like to live in a silent world, but he guessed it could be lonely being cut off from ordinary sounds that hearing people took for granted.

A muscle tightened in Aksel's jaw. He did not want to admire Mina, and he did not want to take her to the cabin. She was a dangerous threat to his peace of mind, especially when he could not forget the searing passion that had burned out of control between them last night. With a curse he slammed the rear door and climbed behind the wheel to drive the last part of the journey that could be made in the four-by-four.

'Where are we?' Mina asked as she climbed out of the truck and caught hold of Aksel's arm to make him turn around so that she could see his face. They had arrived at a building that had suddenly loomed out of the snow and seemed to be in the middle of nowhere. Aksel had driven the four-by-four inside the building, and the light from of the car's headlamps revealed that they were in some sort of warehouse. The place wasn't heated and Mina was already shivering from the bone-biting cold.

'This is as far as we can go by road. From here we'll be travelling on the snowmobile.' He pointed to a contraption that looked like a motorbike on skis.

Travelling to where? Mina wondered. She eyed the snowmobile nervously. 'You expect me to ride on that?'

'I didn't expect you to be here at all.' Aksel spoke carefully so that Mina could read his lips. The glitter in his ice-blue eyes warned her that he was furious with her. He strode over to a cupboard and pulled out several items of clothing, and then walked back to stand in front of her so that she could see his face. 'Luckily my sister keeps spare gear here for emergencies.'

Mina seized this tiny snippet of information about the man who had shared his body with her but nothing else. 'I didn't know you have a sister.'

'There are a lot of things you don't know about me.' He ignored her curiosity and handed her the clothes. 'Put a couple of sweatshirts on under the snowsuit. The more layers you wear, the warmer you'll be.'

Mina doubted she would ever feel warm again. She had to take her skirt off before she could step into the snowsuit and her numb fingers would not work properly. But at last she pulled her boots back on and Aksel handed her a crash helmet. He swung his leg over the saddle of the snowmobile and indicated that she should climb up behind him.

'What if I fall off?' she asked worriedly.

'Then you'll be left behind,' was his uncompromising reply, before he closed the visors on both their helmets and cut off communication between them.

Mina had never been so scared in her life, as Aksel drove the snowmobile across the icy wasteland that stretched endlessly in all directions. There was a grab-rail behind her seat, but she felt safer with her arms wrapped around his waist. At least if she fell off he would be aware of it and might stop.

It had stopped snowing, but the freezing air temperature even through the snowsuit made her blood feel as if it had frozen in her veins. The wind rushed past as the snowmobile picked up speed, and she squeezed her eyes shut and clung to Aksel. His muscular body was reassuringly strong and powerful, and an image flitted into Mina's mind of him naked; his golden-skinned chest crushing her breasts, and his massive arousal pushing between her thighs. Her fear faded and she put her trust in the giant Viking who was confidently steering the snow bike across the ice.

In the light from the snowmobile's headlamp the snow was brilliant white, and above them the vast black sky was crowded with more stars than Mina had known existed. The birch forest became sparser the higher into the mountains they went, and at last a log cabin with lights blazing in the windows came into view.

Mina was relieved to see a house, thinking that she would be able to charge her hearing-aid batteries. She always carried the charger with her but the device needed to be plugged into an electricity supply to work.

As Aksel helped her climb off the bike a strange-looking man stepped out of the shadows. He was wearing what looked like a traditional costume, with an animal hide draped around his shoulders. Mina watched him and Aksel talking and could tell that they were not speaking English or any other language she recognised.

'His name is Isku,' Aksel told her when the man got onto a sledge pulled by huskies and drove off into the night. Mina could feel the vibration of the dogs racing across the snow long after they had disappeared from sight. 'His people are called the Sami. They are reindeer herders and still live according to their ancient traditions. Isku's family are camping near here, and he came to the cabin to light the boiler and make a fire.'

Mina was thankful that Aksel hadn't planned to camp out in the sub-zero temperature. The log cabin looked well built to withstand the Arctic storms. Snow was piled high on the roof and a wisp of grey smoke curled up from the chimney. 'It's so pretty,' she murmured. 'It reminds me of the fairy-tale cottage of the Three Bears.'

Aksel unstrapped the bags from the back of the bike

and remembered to turn to her so that she could watch his mouth as he replied. 'There are no brown bears in Storvhal, and it is very rare that polar bears come this high into the mountains. Their territory is lower down near the coast. The largest predators you might see near the house are wolves.'

He noticed the fearful expression in her eyes as she hurried inside and thought it was probably a good thing she could not hear the howling of wolves close by.

Inside the cabin, a fire blazed in the hearth. Mina quickly started to overheat and had to strip out of the snowsuit and the layers of sweatshirts Aksel had lent her. Her face was flushed by the time she was down to her own shirt, and only then did she realise that she must have left her skirt in the four-by-four where she had got changed.

Aksel pulled off his boots and ski jacket and strode over to the drinks cabinet, where he sloshed neat spirit into a glass and gulped it down, savouring the fiery heat at the back of his throat. He glanced at Mina undressing in front of the fire and felt a tightening sensation in his groin. He recognised her shirt was the same one he had peeled from her body at the hotel in London the previous night. God knew where her skirt was, but he wished she would hurry up and put it on because the shirt only fell to her hips, leaving the creamy skin of her bare thighs above the lace band of her stockings exposed.

With her auburn hair tumbling around her shoulders, and her huge green eyes fixed on him, she was incredibly sensual, and Aksel wanted to forget that he was a prince and kiss her until she pleaded with him to pull her down onto the rug and strip off the remainder of her clothes.

He picked up a second glass and the bottle of liqueur

and walked over to join her in front of the fireplace. 'Here.' He half filled the glass and handed it to her.

Mina took a cautious sip of the straw-coloured liquid and choked. 'That's strong! What is it?'

'*Akevitt* is a traditional Scandinavian spirit. The Storvhalian version is flavoured with aniseed.'

A few sips of the fearsome drink would be likely to render her unconscious, Mina thought. She put the glass down on a table and took the battery charger out of her handbag.

'I need to plug this into an electrical socket to recharge the batteries for my hearing aids.'

Aksel frowned. 'There is no electricity at the cabin. The lamps are filled with oil, and the wood-burning stove heats the hot-water tank. The only modern convenience I keep here is a satellite phone so that my ministers can contact me if necessary. Don't you carry spare batteries for your hearing aids?'

'Both the sets I have with me are dead.' Mina had not anticipated being without her hearing aids. Her degree of hearing loss that she could hear certain sounds above a high decibel, but even if Aksel shouted at the top of his voice she would be unable to hear him. She chewed on her lower lip. 'I'm sorry I've spoiled your trip, but I'm going to have to ask you to take me back to civilisation.'

He shrugged. 'I can't take you anywhere. The heavy snowfall will have blocked the roads further down the valley, and it's snowing again.'

Aksel folded his arms across his chest and a nerve flickered in his jaw as he surveyed her half-undressed state. 'We could be trapped here for days,' he told her grimly.

CHAPTER SIX

MINA'S HEART SANK as she looked over to the window and saw the blizzard that was raging outside. Evidently they had reached the cabin just in time before the weather worsened.

Aksel slid his hand beneath her chin and tilted her face to his so that she could read his lips. 'Why did you come to Storvhal?'

Mina might not be able to hear the anger in his voice, but the rigid set of his jaw was an indication that his temper was on a tight leash. She had as much right to be angry about the photographs in the newspapers as him, she thought, her own temper flaring. His royal status had made them both a target for the paparazzi.

She focused on his question and decided to be honest. 'Before we left the hotel this morning you asked me to meet you in Paris.'

She paused, hoping that her voice did not sound too quiet or flat-toned. She felt self-conscious not being able to hear herself when she spoke, but speech therapy had taught her breathing techniques, and she took a steadying breath before continuing.

'You said that when we made love it had been perfect.' She stared into his eyes, daring him to deny it. 'But later, at the theatre, why did you walk away without listening to me?'

His eyes blazed. 'You tipped off the press that we spent the night together and used me for a publicity stunt. You know damn well the media hype that you are having an affair with a prince will raise your profile when you perform *Romeo and Juliet* in New York.'

Aksel's nostrils flared with the effort of controlling his anger. 'The journalist who was waiting for us outside the hotel this morning was the man I saw you looking at in the pub. He called out your name. You obviously know him so don't try to deny it.'

'His name is Steve Garratt.' Disdain for the journalist flickered across Mina's face. 'It's true that I recognised him when he came into the pub, but he's not a friend— in fact he's the reason I left early. I hate Garratt after he wrote a load of lies about me.'

She bit her lip. 'I know your PA has dug up all that regurgitated rubbish about my supposed affair with Dexter Price, but most of what has been written about me is untrue. I had no idea that Dexter was married or that his wife was ill. He had told me he was divorced and we grew close while we were working on a film in LA. But Steve Garratt accused me of having a torrid affair with him and made me out to be an unscrupulous marriage-wrecker.' Memories of how hurt and humiliated she had been left feeling by the journalist's assassination of her character, and by Dexter Price's refusal to defend her, churned inside Mina.

'No one ever listens to me,' she burst out. 'Not the press, or my father—or you. I may be deaf but that doesn't mean you can ignore me. I didn't tell *anyone* that you had invited me to your hotel. I didn't know when I met you that you are a prince.'

She wished her hearing aids were working. Standing close to Aksel and looking directly at his face so that she could read his lips created an intense atmosphere between them.

'You were just a man,' she said huskily, 'a handsome stranger. I couldn't take my eyes off you and I agreed to go to your hotel because you…overwhelmed me. Making love with you was the most beautiful experience I've ever had, and I…I thought it might have been special for you too—not just a one-night stand—because you asked me to spend a weekend in Paris with you.'

'It wasn't special.' Aksel ignored the stab of guilt he felt when he saw Mina's green eyes darken with hurt. He had been convinced that she had tipped off the press, but now he was beginning to wonder if he might have been wrong about her. Mina's feeling of disgust for the journalist who had taken photos of them outside the hotel had been evident on her expressive features. However, he reminded himself that she was a talented actress. And his instincts were not infallible. Once he had trusted Karena, he remembered grimly.

'Having sex with you was an enjoyable experience, but it was just sex,' he said bluntly, 'and I can't pretend that last night was anything more than a few hours of physical pleasure.'

It felt brutal to look into her eyes as he spoke such harsh words. Usually when he gave women the brush-off he avoided eye contact with them, he acknowledged with savage self-derision.

'Look…' He raked a hand through his hair, feeling unnerved by Mina's intent gaze. He felt as though she could see into his soul—and that was a dark place he never allowed anyone access to. He wanted to step away and put some space between them, but she needed to read his lips.

'I was carried away by the play. When I saw you on stage I was captivated by Juliet.' A nerve flickered in his jaw again. 'But Juliet isn't real—the woman I saw on stage was make-believe. It was my mistake to have forgotten that fact when we met in the pub.'

It was the only explanation Aksel could find for his behaviour that had been so out of character. In all the years he had been Storvhal's monarch he had never picked up a woman in a bar, never done anything to risk damaging his reputation as a responsible, moral prince who was the exact opposite of his father.

Helvete, he had even hidden his son's brief existence for the sake of the Crown. The secret gnawed like a cancer deep in Aksel's heart.

'I made love to Juliet,' he said, speaking carefully so that Mina would not mistake his words. 'For one night I forgot that I belong to an ancient royal dynasty. I was— as you said—just a man who desired a beautiful woman. But in the morning the fantasy ended. You are an actress, and I am a prince and ruler of my country. Our lives are set to follow different paths.'

Mina flinched at his bluntness. She had told herself she had come to Storvhal to clear her name and persuade Aksel that she had not told the press they had spent the night together. But in her heart she knew that her real reason for finding him was because she had felt a deep connection with him when they had made love, and she had been convinced that he had felt it too. His cold words seemed to disprove her theory.

'In that case why did you invite me to Paris?' she said stiffly.

'You looked upset when I told you that I was about to fly back to Storvhal. It seemed kinder to allow you to believe that I was interested in seeing you again, but we hadn't made a specific arrangement.'

Humiliation swept in a hot tide through Mina. Fool, she silently berated herself. She went cold when she remembered that Aksel had called her Juliet when he had kissed her. At the time she hadn't thought anything of it, but now she knew that he had been making love to a fantasy woman. He had been captivated by Juliet when he had watched her on stage, not by Mina Hart, the actress who played the role. According to Aksel, he hadn't felt any kind of connection to her. She had completely misread the situation.

Or had she?

Her mind flew back to the previous night, and the fierce glitter in Aksel's eyes just before he had climaxed powerfully inside her. For a few timeless moments when they had both hovered on the edge of heaven, she had sensed that their souls had reached out to each other and something indefinable and profound had passed between them.

Last night her hearing aids had been working. Could Aksel really have faked the raw emotion she had heard in the groan he'd made when he had come apart in her arms?

He lifted his glass to his lips and gulped down the fiery *akevitt* in a single swallow. For a split second, Mina saw him flick his gaze over her in a lightning sweep from her breasts down to her stocking tops, and she glimpsed a predatory hunger in his eyes before he glanced away.

Her heart thudded. Aksel might want to deny that he felt anything for her, but she had seen desire in his eyes. She couldn't shake off the feeling that when they had made love the previous night it *had* been special. She had not imagined his tenderness and she was convinced that they had shared more than a primitive physical act.

If he had spoken the truth when he'd stated that he'd just wanted sex with her, why hadn't he looked into her eyes as he had said it? And why was he still determined to avoid her gaze? Mina was adept at reading the subtle nuances of body language, and the tension she could feel emanating from Aksel suggested that he was not telling her the whole truth.

'So, you desired the fantasy Juliet, not Mina the real woman?' she demanded. When he did not look at her she put her hand on his jaw and felt the rough stubble scrape her palm as she turned his face towards her. His eyelashes swept down, but not before she had glimpsed something in his eyes that gave her courage. 'Prove it,' she said softly.

His dark blond brows drew together. 'What do you mean?'

'Kiss me and prove that I don't turn you on.'

'Don't be ridiculous.'

She stood up on tiptoe and brought her face so close to his that when he blinked she felt his eyelashes brush her skin. Being deprived of her hearing made her other senses more acute and she was aware of the unsteady rhythm of his heart as his breathing became shallow.

'What are you afraid of?' she said against his mouth. 'If I kiss you and you don't respond, then I'll know you're telling the truth and you don't want me.'

Are you crazy? taunted a voice inside her head. You won't dare do it! If he rejected her she would die of humiliation. But life had taught Mina that if you wanted something badly enough it was worth fighting for.

If she could only break through Aksel's icy detachment, she was convinced she would find the tender lover he had been last night. She hesitated with her lips centimetres from his and felt his warm breath whisper across her skin. He had tensed, but he hadn't pushed her away, and before she lost her nerve she closed the tiny gap between them and grazed her mouth over Aksel's.

He made no response, not even when she pressed her lips harder against his and traced the shape of his mouth with the tip of her tongue. Desperation gripped her and she began to wonder if last night really had been just a casual sexual encounter for him.

He stood unmoving, as unrelenting as rock, and in frustration she nipped his lower lip with her teeth. His chest lifted as he inhaled sharply, and Mina took advantage of his surprise to push her tongue into his mouth.

He curled his hands around her shoulders and tightened his grip until his fingers bit into her flesh. Mina tensed, expecting him to wrench his mouth free and cast her from him. But suddenly, unbelievably, he was kissing her back.

He moved his mouth over hers, tentatively at first—as if he was still fighting a battle with himself. Relief flooded through Mina and she pressed her body closer to him so that her breasts were crushed against the hard wall of his chest. And all the while she moved her lips over his with aching sensuality, teasing him, tempting him, until Aksel could withstand no more of the sweet torture.

A shudder ran through his huge frame. He loosened his grip on her shoulders and grabbed a fistful of her hair, holding her captive while he demonstrated his mastery and claimed control of the kiss.

It was no slow build-up of passion but a violent explosion that set them both on fire. Mina wondered if her bones would be crushed by Aksel's immense strength as he hauled her hard against him. But she did not care. His raw hunger made her melt into him as she responded to his demanding kisses with demands of her own. She curled her fingers into his hair and shaped his skull before tracing her fingertips over his sculpted face and the blond stubble covering his jaw.

He lifted her up and she wrapped her legs around his waist while he strode through the cabin and into the bedroom. Mina was vaguely aware of a fire burning in the hearth, and an oil lamp hanging on the wall cast a pool of golden light on the bed. The mattress dipped as Aksel laid her down and knelt over her. His eyes were no longer icy but blazed with desire that matched the molten heat coursing through Mina's veins.

She felt fiercely triumphant that her feminine instinct had been right and he wanted *her*. His excuse that he had desired the fantasy Juliet was patently untrue. The erratic thud of his heart gave him away, and his hands were unsteady as he tore open her shirt and pushed it over her shoulders. He slipped a hand beneath her back to unfasten her bra and tugged away the wisp of lace to lay bare her breasts. Mina watched streaks of dull colour flare on his sharp cheekbones, and, even before he had touched her breasts, her nipples tautened in response to the feral gleam in his eyes.

Aksel lifted his head and stared down at Mina. 'You are driving me insane, you green-eyed witch.'

She read his lips and smiled. 'Who am I?'

He frowned. 'You're Mina.'

'Not Juliet?'

Now he understood. 'You're a witch,' he repeated. She made him forget his royal status and his life of responsibility and duty. She made him forget everything but his urgent, scalding need that was unlike anything he'd ever felt for any other woman. He cupped her firm breasts in his hands and flicked his thumb pads across the puckered nipples, smiling when he heard her sharp intake of breath that told him her hunger was as acute as his.

Mina gave a choked cry as Aksel kissed her breasts, transferring his mouth from one nipple to the other and lashing the swollen peaks with his tongue until the pleasure was almost unbearable. She could feel his erection straining beneath his jeans and she fumbled with his zip, eager to take him inside her. There was something excitingly primitive about the way he jerked the denim over his hips; the fact that he was too impatient to possess her to undress properly.

She wrenched his shirt buttons open and spread the material so that she could run her hands through the wiry blond hairs that grew on his chest. He dragged her knickers down her legs, and then his big hand was between her thighs, spreading her wide, touching her where she ached to be touched.

Mina closed her eyes and fell into a dark, silent world where her other senses dominated. The feel of Aksel parting her and sliding a finger into her wetness was almost enough to make her come. She could smell his male scent; spicy aftershave mingled with the faint saltiness of sweaty and the indefinable fragrance of sexual arousal. When he moved his hand she arched her hips in mute supplication for him to push his finger deeper inside her.

It wasn't enough, not nearly enough. She curled her hand around his powerful erection and gave a little shiver of excitement when she remembered how he had filled her last night. She lifted her lashes and studied his chiselled features, and her heart stirred. He wasn't a stranger, she had known him for ever, and she wondered why she suddenly felt shy and nervous and excited all at the same time. She smiled, unaware that her eyes mirrored her confused feelings of hope and anticipation, but Aksel tensed, and silently cursed his stupidity.

Reality struck him forcibly. There were numerous reasons why he must not allow the situation to continue, but the most crucial was that he could not have unprotected sex with Mina. He never brought women to his private sanctuary and he did not keep condoms at the cabin. Perhaps Mina used a method of contraception, but years ago Karena had told him she was on the pill, and since then he had never trusted any woman. His gut ached with sexual frustration but, even though he was agonisingly tempted to plunge his throbbing erection between her soft thighs, he could not, would not, take the risk of making Mina pregnant.

A series of images flashed into his mind. He remembered looking into Finn's crib and pulling back the blanket that was half covering the baby's face. At first he had thought that his son was asleep. He'd looked so peaceful with his long eyelashes curling on his cheeks. The baby's skin was as flawless as fine porcelain—*but his little cheek had felt as cold as marble.*

Pain tore in Aksel's chest as he snatched a breath and forced air into his lungs that felt as though they had been crushed in a vice. There were other reasons why he should resist the siren call of Mina's body, not least the soft expression in her eyes that was a warning sign she hoped for something more from him than sex. He needed to make her understand that nothing was on offer. His emotions were as cold and empty as the Arctic tundra.

'Don't stop,' she murmured. Her words affected Aksel more than he cared to admit. He wondered if she could hear her own voice, or whether she was unaware of the husky pleading in her tone. He looked down at her slender body spread naked on his bed and could not bring himself to reject her when she was at her most vulnerable.

Helvete! How had he allowed things to get this far? He should have tried harder to resist her, but the sweet sensuality of her kiss had driven him out of his mind. She looped her arms around his neck and pulled his head down, parting her lips in an invitation that Aksel found he could not ignore. He slanted his mouth over hers, and desire ripped through him when he tasted her warm breath in his mouth.

She twisted her hips restlessly, pushing her sex against his hand. It would be cruel to deny her what she clearly wanted, Aksel told himself. He could give her pleasure even if he could give her nothing else.

The little moan she made when he slipped a second finger inside her and moved his hand in a rhythmic dance told him she was close to the edge. He forced himself to ignore the burn of his own desire and concentrated on Mina. Her head was thrown back on the pillows, her glorious hair spilling around her shoulders, and she closed her eyes as tremors shook her body.

'Aksel...' Her keening cry tugged on his heart. He did not understand why he wanted to gather her close and rock her in his arms while the trembling in her limbs gradually eased. The sight of tears sliding from beneath her lashes filled him with self-loathing. She had flown all the way to Storvhal to find him because—in her words— she believed that last night had been special for both of them. The brutal truth was going to hurt her feelings, he acknowledged grimly as he withdrew from her.

Mina watched Aksel get up from the bed, and the languorous feeling following her orgasm turned to excitement as she waited for him to strip off his jeans and position himself over her. Despite the pleasure he had just gifted her she was desperate to take his hard length inside her. She did not recognise the wanton creature she became with him. He had unlocked a deeply sensual side to her nature that she had been unaware of, and she was eager to make love with him fully and give him as much pleasure as he had given her.

But instead of removing the rest of his clothes he was pulling up the zip of his jeans. Her confusion grew when he walked over to the door. She sat up and pushed her hair out of her eyes. 'Aksel...what's wrong?'

He turned around so that she could see his face, and her heart plummeted at the coldness in his eyes. She watched his mouth form words that made no sense to her.

'This is wrong.' His eyes rested on her slender figure and rose-flushed face. 'You should not have come to Storvhal.'

Mina felt sick as the realisation sank in that he was rejecting her. 'Last night—' she began. But he cut her off.

'Last night was a mistake that I am not going to repeat.'

'Why?' Mina was unaware of the raw emotion in her voice, and Aksel schooled his features to hide the pang of guilt he felt.

She bit her lip. Her pride demanded that she should accept his rejection and try to salvage a little of her dignity, but she did not understand why he had suddenly backed off. 'Is it because I'm deaf? You desired me when you didn't know about my hearing loss,' she reminded him when he frowned. 'What am I supposed to blame for your sudden change of heart?'

'My heart was never involved,' he said bluntly. 'Learning of your hearing impairment is not the reason why I can't have sex with you again.'

'Then what is the reason?' The frustration Mina had felt as a child when she had first lost her hearing surged through her again now. She wished she could hear Aksel. It wasn't that she had a problem reading his lip, but not being able to hear his voice made her feel that there was a wide gulf between them.

'I can't have an affair with you. I am the Prince of Storvhal and my loyalty and duty must be to my country.'

Mina suddenly felt self-conscious that he was dressed and she was naked when she noticed his gaze linger on her breasts. She flushed as she glanced down at her swollen nipples—evidence that her body had still not come down from the sexual high he had taken her to—and tugged a sheet around her before she slid off the bed and walked towards him.

'I understand that you have many responsibilities.' She remembered the taxi driver saying that Aksel had needed to win the support of the Storvhalian people after his father had been an unpopular ruler. Aksel had admitted that, when they had made love last night, he had been able to briefly forget his royal status.

'You belong to an ancient royal dynasty, but surely the Storvhalian people accept that you are a man first, and a prince second?' she said softly.

She was shocked to see a flash of emotion in his eyes, but it disappeared before she could define it, and she wondered if she had imagined his expression of raw pain.

Aksel grimaced as he imagined how his grandmother would react to Mina's lack of understanding of his role as ruler of Storvhal. It was a role he had prepared for probably since he had taken his first steps. He remembered when he was a small boy, Princess Eldrun had insisted that he must not run through the palace but must walk sedately as befitted the future monarch. His whole life had been constrained by strict rules of protocol, and he had done his best to fulfil the expectations that his grandmother, his government ministers—the entire nation of Storvhal, it often felt like—had of him.

He had even kept secret his son's birth—and death.

He stared at Mina and hardened his heart against the

temptation of her beauty. 'I swore an oath promising my devotion to my country and my people. I will always be a prince first.'

'Do you place duty above everything because you feel you have to make up for the fact that your father wasn't a good monarch?'

He stiffened. 'How do you know anything about my father?'

She gave a wry smile. 'My father says that if you want to hear an honest opinion about politics or any other subject, talk to a taxi driver.'

The gentle expression in Mina's green eyes infuriated Aksel. She did not understand anything about his life. *The sacrifice he had made that would haunt him for ever.*

'Did the taxi driver you spoke to tell you that during my father's reign many of his own ministers supported a move to abolish the monarchy? There were incidents of civil unrest among the population and the House of Thoresen, who have ruled Storvhal for eight centuries, came close to being overthrown.

'My father betrayed Storvhal by selling off gold reserves and other valuable assets belonging to the country to fund his extravagant lifestyle. He was called the playboy prince for good reason and the Storvhalian population disliked that their ruler was setting a bad moral example.

'It has taken twelve years for me to win back the trust of my people.' Anger flashed in Aksel's eyes. 'But now, thanks to your wretched journalist friend and the photographs of me escorting an actress with a dubious reputation into my hotel, rumours abound that I lead a secret double life and I am a playboy like my father.'

Aksel knew as soon as he spoke that he was being unfair. The real blame lay with him. God knew what he had been thinking of when he had invited Mina to his hotel last night. The truth was he hadn't been thinking at all. He had been bewitched by a green-eyed sorceress and risked his reputation and the support of the Storvhalian people to satisfy his sexual desire for a woman whose own reputation, it turned out, was hardly without blemish.

Mina blanched as she read Aksel's lips. How dared he judge her based on what he had read about her in the newspapers? Good grief, she had only ever had one sexual relationship—two if she counted Aksel, she amended. But one night in his bed did not constitute a relationship—as he seemed determined to make clear. The unfairness brought tears to her eyes.

'At the risk of repeating myself, I didn't tell the press about us,' she said tautly. 'I discovered from bitter experience that the paparazzi prefer to print scandal and lies than the truth.'

Even with her talent for acting, could she really sound so convincing if she was lying? Aksel wondered. He had found the newspaper article about her affair with a married film director distasteful, but, hell, the paparazzi could make a vicar's tea party sound sordid.

Glimpsing the shimmer of her tears made him feel even more of a bastard than he'd felt when he had stopped making love to her. He wanted to look away before he drowned in her deep green eyes, but he forced himself to remain facing her so that she could watch his lips when he spoke.

'You should get some sleep. As soon as there's a break in the weather I want to get us off the mountain, and that might mean I'll have to wake you early in the morning. Put another log on the fire before you get into bed and you should be warm enough.'

'What about you?' Mina stopped him as he went to walk out of the room. 'Where are you going to sleep?'

'I'll make up a bed on the sofa in the living room.'

'I feel bad that I've taken your bed.' She hesitated, and glanced at the huge wooden-framed bed. 'It's a big bed and I don't mind sharing.'

'But I do.'

His glinting gaze made Mina feel sure he was mocking her. She flushed. 'Don't worry. I'd keep to my side of the mattress.'

He turned his head away, but not before her sharp eyes read the words on his lips that he had spoken to himself. 'I wish I could be certain that I could keep my hands off you, my green-eyed temptress.'

Mina felt confused as she watched him walk into the living room and pick up the bottle of fiery liqueur *akevitt* before he sprawled on the rug in front of the fire. She had not imagined the feral hunger in his eyes. But Aksel believed that he must put his duty to Storvhal above his personal desires. Perhaps that explained the aching loneliness she had glimpsed, before his lashes had swept down and hidden his expression, she mused as she climbed into the big bed and huddled beneath the covers.

CHAPTER SEVEN

THE FLAMES IN the hearth were leaping high into the chimney when Mina woke. The fire had burned down to embers during the night and she guessed that Aksel had thrown on more logs while she was sleeping. She slid out of bed and pulled back the curtains. It was not snowing at the moment, but the towering grey clouds looked ominous and Aksel's warning that they could be trapped at the cabin for days seemed entirely possible.

Although her watch showed that it was nine a.m. it was barely light. By the end of the month it would be polar night and the sun would not rise above the horizon until next year. The land was an Arctic wilderness: remote, beautiful and icy cold—a description that equally fitted the Prince of Storvhal, Mina thought ruefully.

A movement caught her attention, and she turned her head to see Aksel at the side of the house chopping logs with an axe. Despite the freezing temperature he was only dressed in jeans and a sweater. He paused for a moment to push his blond hair out of his eyes, and Mina's heart-rate quickened as she studied his powerful body. There was not an ounce of spare flesh on his lean hips, and his thigh muscles rippled beneath his jeans as he dropped the axe and gathered up an armful of logs.

Mina often rued her impulsive nature, but she could

not resist opening the window and scooping up a handful of snow from the ledge. She took aim, and the snowball landed between Aksel's shoulder blades. He jerked upright, and she guessed he shouted something, but he was too far away for her to be able to read his lips. He must have heard her slam the window shut because he spun round and his startled expression brought a smile to her lips. It was heartening to know that he might be a prince but he was also a human being.

Having not brought any spare clothes with her, she had no alternative but to put on Aksel's shirt that he had taken off when he had started to make love to her the previous night. The shirt came to midway down her thighs and, feeling reassured that she was at least half decently covered, she made a quick exploration of the cabin. She entered the large kitchen at the same moment that Aksel walked in through the back door, and stopped dead when she saw a snowball in his hands and a determined gleam in his eyes.

'*No…!*' She dodged too late and gave a yelp as the snowball landed in the centre of her chest. 'Don't you dare…!' Face alight with laughter, she backed away from him, her eyes widening when she saw he was holding a second snowball. She raced around the table but he caught her easily and grinned wickedly as he shoved snow down the front of her shirt.

'*Oh*…that's cold.' She gasped as the melting snow trickled down her breasts.

He slid his hand beneath her chin and tilted her face so that she could watch him speak. Amusement warmed his ice-blue eyes. 'You asked for it, angel.'

'That wasn't fair to bring snow into the house. Don't you know the rules of snowball fights?'

He shook his head. 'I've never had a snowball fight.'

'Never?' Mina stared out of the window at the snowy landscape. 'But you live in a land of snow and ice. When you were a child you must have had snowball fights with the other kids at school, and surely you built snowmen?'

'I didn't go to school, and I rarely played with other children.'

She could not hide her surprise. 'That's...sad. I know you are a prince, but in England the children of the royal family are educated at school. Didn't your parents think it was important for you to mix with other children of your own age?'

Aksel's smile faded at Mina's curiosity. 'My grandmother supervised my upbringing because my parents were busy with their own lives. I was taught by excellent tutors at the palace until I went to university when I was eighteen.'

The few years he had spent in England at Cambridge University had been the happiest of his life, Aksel thought to himself. He had enjoyed socialising with the other students who came from different backgrounds, and he had loved the sense of freedom and being able to lead a normal life away from the protocol of the palace. Even the press had left him alone, but that had all changed when his father had died and the new Prince of Storvhal had been thrust into the public spotlight.

Mina recalled something the taxi driver had told her. 'I heard that your mother is Russian, but the people of Storvhal didn't approve of your father's choice of bride.'

'Historically there was often tension between my country and Russia. Seventy years ago my grandfather signed a treaty with Norway, which means that the principality of Storvhal is protected by the Norwegian military.'

Aksel shrugged. 'It is true that my father's marriage

to my mother was not popular, particularly as my mother made it plain that she disliked Storvhal and preferred to be in Moscow. I grew up at the palace with my grandmother. My father spent most of his time with his many mistresses in the French Riviera, and I did not see either of my parents very often.'

Aksel's explanation that his grandmother had 'supervised' his upbringing gave Mina the impression that his childhood had been lacking love and affection. She pictured him as a solemn-faced little boy playing on his own in the vast royal palace.

'You said you have a sister.' She remembered he had mentioned a sibling.

'Linne is ten years younger than me, and she lived mainly with my mother. We were not close as children, although we have a good relationship now.'

'Does your sister live at the palace?'

'Sometimes, but at the moment she is on an Arctic research ship in Alaska. Linne is a glaciologist, which is the subject I studied at university before I had to return to Storvhal to rule the country.'

Although Mina could not hear Aksel's tone of voice, years of experience at lip-reading had given her a special understanding of body language and she glimpsed a hint of regret in his eyes. 'Do you wish you were a scientist rather than a prince?' she asked intuitively.

His expression became unreadable. 'It does not matter what I wish for. It was my destiny to be a prince and it is my duty to rule to the best of my ability.'

Mina nodded thoughtfully. 'I think you must have had a lonely childhood. I know what that feels like. My parents decided to send me to a mainstream school where I was the only deaf child, and I always felt apart from the other children because I was different. My sister was the only person who really understood how I struggled to fit in with my peers.' She gave a rueful smile. 'I don't know how I would have managed without Darcey. She was my best friend and my protector against the other kids who used to call me dumb because I was shy of speaking.'

Aksel gave her a puzzled look. 'In that case, why did you choose to become an actress?'

'All my family are actors. My father is often called the greatest Shakespearean actor of all times, but my mother is also amazingly talented. Performing in front of an audience is in my blood and I decided that I wasn't going to allow my loss of hearing to alter who I am or affect my choice of career.'

Mina sighed. 'I suppose I was determined to prove to my father that I could be a good actress despite being deaf. Dad was supportive, but I know he doubted that I would be able to go on the stage. I wanted to make him proud of me. But at the moment, he's furious,' she said ruefully, remembering Joshua Hart's explosive temper when she had met him at the Globe Theatre after she had spent the night with Aksel.

'Why is your father angry with you?' Why the hell did he care? Aksel asked himself impatiently. He told himself he did not want to hear about Mina's life, but he could not dismiss the image of her as a little girl, struggling to cope with her hearing impairment and feeling ostracised by the other pupils at school. He was glad her sister had stood up for her.

'Joshua was not impressed to see a photograph of me with a prince, and details about my supposed love-life, splashed across the front pages of the newspapers. I am his daughter and the lead actress in his production of *Romeo and Juliet*, and he feels that any sort of scandal will reflect badly on the Hart family and on the play.' She bit her lip. 'He accused me of turning Shakespeare into a soap opera.'

Aksel frowned. 'Surely you told him it was not your fault that you were snapped by the paparazzi?'

'Of course I did—but like you he didn't believe me,' Mina said drily.

Aksel's jaw clenched. He felt an inexplicable anger with Mina's father and wanted to confront Joshua Hart and tell him that he should be supportive of his beautiful and talented daughter, who had faced huge challenges after she had lost her hearing, with immense courage.

He stared at Mina and felt a fierce rush of desire at the sight of her wet shirt—his shirt—clinging to her breasts. The melting snowball had caused her nipples to stand erect and he could see the hard tips and the dark pink aureoles jutting beneath the fine cotton shirt.

Helvete! She had thrown what he had planned to be a peaceful weekend into turmoil and the sooner he could take her back down the mountain, the better for his peace of mind.

'Linne left some spare clothes in the wardrobe. Help yourself to what you need. There's plenty of hot water if you want a shower, and food in the larder, if you're hungry.' He grabbed his jacket. 'I'm going for a walk.'

'Do you think that's a good idea? It's snowing again.'

Aksel followed her gaze to the window and saw swirling white snowflakes falling from the sky. This was the last time he would come to the cabin before winter set in and he might not get another chance to visit his son's grave. He could not explain to Mina that sometimes he craved the solitude of the mountains.

'I won't be long,' he told her, and quickly turned away from her haunting deep green gaze.

* * *

The pair of jeans and a thick woollen jumper belonging to Aksel's sister that she found in the wardrobe fitted Mina perfectly. With no hairdrier, she had to leave her hair to dry into natural loose waves rather than the sleek style she preferred. The only item of make-up she kept in her handbag was a tube of lip gloss. She wondered ruefully if Aksel liked the fresh-faced, girl-next-door look, and reminded herself that it did not matter what she looked like because he had made it quite clear that he regretted sleeping with her and had no intention of doing so again.

Returning to the kitchen, she found rye bread, cheese and ham in the larder. There was no electricity at the cabin to power a fridge, but the walk-in larder was as cold as a freezer. She could see no sign of Aksel when she peered through the window that was half covered by ice. His footprints had long since been obliterated by the falling snow and in every direction stretched a barren, white wasteland.

It was more than two hours later when she spotted him striding towards the cabin through snow that reached to his mid-thighs. He stripped out of his snowsuit and boots in the cloakroom and came into the kitchen shaking snow out of his hair. Mina could not control her accelerated heart-rate as she skimmed her eyes over his grey wool sweater that clung to his broad shoulders and chest. His rugged masculinity evoked a sharp tug of desire in the pit of her stomach, but when she studied his face she almost gasped out loud at the bleak expression in his eyes. She wanted to ask him what was wrong—why did he look so *tormented*? But before she could say anything, he walked over to the larder and took out a bottle of *akevitt*, which he opened, and poured a liberal amount of the straw-coloured liqueur into a glass.

She glanced at the kettle on the gas stove. 'I was going to make coffee. Do you want some to warm you up?'

He dropped into a chair opposite her at the table so that she could see his face. His mouth curved into a cynical smile as he lifted his glass. 'This warms my blood better than coffee.'

Mina bit her lip. 'You were gone for a long time. I was starting to worry that something had happened to you.' When he raised his brows, she said quickly, 'You said there are wolves around here.'

'Wolves don't attack humans. In fact they very sensibly try to avoid them. I've been coming to the cabin since I was a teenager, and I know these mountains well.'

'Why do you come to such a remote place?'

He shrugged. 'It's the one place I can be alone, to think.'

'And drink.' Mina watched him take a long swig of the strong spirit, and glanced at the empty liqueur bottle on the draining board that he must have finished last night. 'Drinking alone is a dangerous habit.' She gave him a thoughtful look. 'What are you trying to forget?'

'Nothing.' He stood up abruptly and his chair fell backwards and clattered on the wooden floorboards. 'I come to the cabin for some peace and quiet, but clearly I'm not going to get either with you asking endless questions.'

As she watched him stride out of the room Mina wondered what raw nerve she had touched that had made him react so violently. Aksel gave the impression of being coldly unemotional, but beneath the surface he was a complex man, and she sensed that his emotions ran deep. Had something happened in his past that had caused him to withdraw into himself?

He strode back into the kitchen and leaned over her, capturing her chin in his hand and tilting her head up so she was forced to watch his mouth when he spoke. 'What makes you think you're a damn psychologist?'

'Actually, I have studied psychology, and I am a qualified drama therapist.'

Aksel stared into Mina's eyes and felt his anger drain out of him. She had come too close to the truth for comfort when she had suggested that he drank alcohol as a means of trying to block out the past. It wasn't that he wanted to forget Finn—never that. But sometimes the only way he could cope with the guilt that haunted him was to anaesthetise his pain with alcohol.

He frowned. 'What the hell is a drama therapist?'

'Drama therapy is a form of psychological therapy. Drama therapists use drama and theatre techniques to help clients with a wide range of emotional problems, from adults suffering from dementia through to children who have experienced psychological trauma.' Mina was unaware that her voice became increasingly enthusiastic as she explained about drama therapy, which was a subject close to her heart. 'In my role as a drama therapist, I use stories, role-play, improvisation and puppets—a whole range of artistic devices to enable children to explore difficult and painful life experiences.'

Aksel was curious, despite telling himself that he did not want to become involved with Mina. 'How do you combine being a drama therapist with your acting career?'

'I managed to fit acting work around my drama therapy training, but now that I am a fully qualified therapist I've been thinking about leaving acting to concentrate on a full-time career as a drama therapist.

'I love the stage. I'm a Hart and performing is in my blood. My father would be disappointed if I gave up acting,' Mina admitted. 'But I had been thinking for a while that I would like to do something more meaningful with my life. My sister Darcey trained as a speech therapist after seeing how vital speech therapy was for me when I became deaf. Being ill with meningitis when I was a child and losing my hearing was hugely traumatic. I feel that my experiences have given me an empathy with children who have suffered emotional and physical trauma.

'I didn't become an actress to be famous,' she told Aksel. 'I hate show business and the celebrity culture. When I made that film in America, and the media falsely accused me of having that affair, I saw a side to acting that I don't want to be a part of.

'The photos in the newspapers of me going into a hotel with you and leaving the next morning looking like I'd spent a wild night in your bed are the worst thing that could have happened as far as I'm concerned. The lies written about my relationship with Dexter Price have been reprinted and my reputation is in tatters.' She grimaced. 'You should have been honest when we met, and told me who you are. You might be a prince, but you're not my Prince Charming.'

Aksel's expression was thunderous, but he did not reply. Instead he grabbed the bottle of *akevitt* and walked out of the room, leaving Mina trembling inside and silently calling herself every kind of a fool, because while he had been leaning over her she had ached for him to cover her mouth with his and kiss her until the world went away.

By mid-afternoon the weak sun had slipped below the horizon once more and the snow clouds had been blown away to leave a clear, indigo-coloured sky. Aksel lit the oil lamps, and Mina was curled up in an armchair by the fire, reading. She had been surprised to find that many of the books in the book case were English.

'English is the second official language of Storvhal,' Aksel explained. 'When I became Prince I made it a law that schools must also teach children English. It is important for the population to retain a strong link to their culture, but Storvhal is a small country and we must be able to compete on world markets and communicate using a globally recognised language.'

He lowered his sketch pad where he had been idly drawing, and looked over at Mina. 'Why did your parents send you to a mainstream school?'

'I was eight when I lost my hearing and by that age I had learned speech and language. Mum and Dad were concerned that if I went to a specialist school for deaf children I might lose my verbal skills. But the hearing aids I wore then were not as good as the ones I have now, and I struggled—not so much with my school work, but I found it hard to be accepted by the other children.' She gave a wry smile. 'Luckily I learned to act, and I was good at pretending that I didn't care about being teased. Most people didn't realise that I could lip-read when they called me dumb or stupid.'

'You certainly proved your tormentors wrong by becoming a gifted actress.' Aksel frowned as he imagined the difficulties Mina had faced as a child—and perhaps still sometimes faced as an adult, he mused. She seemed to have no problem understanding him by reading his lips, but he wondered if she felt vulnerable without her hearing aids.

'I'd like to learn more about drama therapy,' he said. 'That type of specialised psychotherapy is not available in Storvhal, but I think it could help a group of children from a fishing village, whose fathers were all drowned when their boats sank during a storm at sea. Twenty families were affected, and the tragedy has touched everyone in the small village of Revika. The local school teachers and community leaders are doing what they can, but the children are devastated.'

'Such a terrible disaster is bound to have left the children deeply traumatised,' Mina murmured. 'Drama therapy could provide a way for the children to explore and express their feelings.'

She gave up trying to concentrate on her book. In truth she had spent more time secretly watching Aksel than reading. In the flickering firelight, his sculpted face was all angles and planes, and she longed to run her fingers through his golden hair.

She glanced at the sketch pad. 'What are you drawing?'

'You.' His answer surprised her.

'Can I see?'

He hesitated, and then shrugged and handed her the pad. Mina's eyes widened as she studied the skilful charcoal sketch of herself. 'You're very good at drawing. Did you study art?'

'Not formally. Drawing is a hobby I began as a child and I'm self-taught.'

Mina handed him back the sketch pad. 'You've made me prettier than I really am.'

'I disagree. I haven't been able to capture your beauty as accurately as I wish I could.'

Her heart leapt, but she firmly told herself she must have made a mistake when she'd read his lips, just as she must have mistaken the reflection of the firelight in his eyes for desire. The atmosphere between them pricked with an undercurrent of tension, and in an attempt to ig-

nore it she turned her attention to a second sketch pad
lying on the table.

'Do you mind if I have a look at your work?'

'Be my guest.'

The drawings were mainly done in charcoal or pencil and were predominantly of wildlife that she guessed
Aksel had spotted in the mountains. There were several
sketches of reindeer, as well as a lynx, an Arctic fox
and some stunningly detailed drawings of wolves. The
sketches were skilfully executed, but they were more
than simply accurate representations of a subject; they
had been drawn with real appreciation for wildlife and
revealed a depth of emotion in Aksel that he kept hidden
in all other aspects of his life.

He was an enigma, Mina thought with a sigh as she
closed the sketch pad. She stood up and carried the pad
over to Aksel to put back on the shelf, but as she handed
it to him a loose page fell out onto the floor. She leaned
down to pick it up, but he moved quickly and snatched
up the drawing. However he had not been quick enough
to prevent Mina from seeing the drawing of a baby. She
guessed the infant was very young, perhaps only a few
weeks old, she mused, thinking of her sister's twin boys
when they had been newborns.

Her eyes flew to Aksel's face. She wanted to ask him
about the drawing—a baby seemed an unusual subject
for him to have sketched. But something in his expression made her hesitate. His granite-hard features showed
no emotion but he seemed strangely tense, and for a second she glimpsed a look of utter bleakness in his eyes
that caused her to take a sharp breath.

'Aksel…?' she said uncertainly.

'Leave it, Mina.'

She could not hear him but she sensed his tone had

been curt. He deliberately turned away from her as he slipped the drawing inside the cover of the sketch pad and placed the book on the shelf.

Her confusion grew when he turned off the oil lamps so that the room was dark, apart from the orange embers of the fire flickering in the hearth. Unable to see Aksel's face clearly to read his lips, Mina stiffened when he put a hand on her shoulder and steered her over to the window. But the sight that met her eyes was so spectacular that everything else flew from her mind.

She had heard about the natural phenomenon known as the aurora borealis but nothing had prepared her for the awe-inspiring light show that filled the sky. Swirling clouds of greens and pinks performed a magical dance. Mystical spirits, shimmering and ethereal, cast an eerie glow that illuminated the sky and reflected rainbow colours on the blanket of white snow beneath.

Mina vaguely recalled, from a geography lesson at school, that the aurora—sometimes called the Northern Lights—were caused by gas particles in the earth's atmosphere colliding, and the most stunning displays could only be seen at the north and south poles. But the reason why the aurora took place did not seem important. She was transfixed by the beauty of nature's incredible display and felt humbled and deeply moved that she was lucky enough to witness something so magnificent. As she stared up at the heavens the tension seeped from her body and she unconsciously leaned back against Aksel's chest.

Aksel drew a ragged breath as he struggled to impose his usual icy control over his emotions. Seeing the picture of Finn had been a shock and he'd felt winded, as though he had been punched in his gut. He hadn't known the drawing was tucked in the sketch pad. He must have put it there years ago, but he remembered sketching his son while the baby had been asleep in his crib.

His little boy had been so beautiful. Aksel took another harsh breath and felt an ache in the back of his throat as he watched the glorious light spectacle outside the window. He had seen the aurora many times but he never failed to be awed by its other-worldly beauty. It gave him some comfort to know that Finn was up here on the mountain. If there was a heaven, then this remote spot, with the aurora lighting up the sky, was surely the closest place to paradise.

He recalled the puzzled expression in Mina's eyes when she had seen the sketch. It had been obvious that she was curious about the identity of the baby. What shocked him was that for a crazy moment he had actually contemplated telling her about Finn.

He frowned. Why would he reveal his deepest secret to her when he was not certain that he could trust her? Why, after so many years of carrying his secret alone, did he long to unburden his soul to this woman? Perhaps it was because he recognised her compassion, he brooded. How many people would choose to give up a successful acting career to become a psychotherapist working with traumatised children?

But he doubted Mina would be sympathetic if he revealed the terrible thing he had done. For eight years he had hidden his son's birth from the Storvhalian people, his friends, and even from his grandmother. He had believed he was doing the best thing for the monarchy, but his guilt ate away at him. He did not deserve Mina's compassion, and he had not deserved her mind-blowing sensuality when they had made love.

His mind flew back to two nights ago, and the memory of her generosity and eagerness to please him caused subtle warmth to flow through his veins, melting the ice inside him. He became aware of her bottom pressing against his thighs and an image came into his mind of the peachy perfection of her bare buttocks. The warmth in his veins turned to searing heat and the throb of desire provided a temporary respite from the dull ache of grief in his heart.

In the darkened room he could see the profile of her lovely face and the slender column of her throat. Last night it had taken all his will power to walk away from her, but right now, when his emotions felt raw, it was becoming harder to remember why he must resist her.

He wanted to press his lips to her white neck, wanted it so badly that his fingers clenched and bit into her shoulder, causing her to make a startled protest. She turned her head towards him and her mouth was mere centimetres from his, offering an unbearable temptation. Surely there was no harm in kissing her? He felt a tremor run through her and knew she was waiting for him to claim her lips. He dipped his head lower so that his mouth almost grazed hers. One kiss was all he would take, he told himself.

One kiss would not be enough, a voice inside his head taunted. If he kissed her he would be bewitched by her sensual magic. But the reason he had fought his desire for her last night had not changed. He could not have unprotected sex with her and risk her conceiving his child. Nor would it be fair to allow her to think that he wanted a relationship with her. The brutal truth was that he wanted to lose himself in her softness and forget temporarily the past that haunted him.

Mina stumbled as Aksel snatched his hand from her shoulder. She did not know what had happened to make him move abruptly away from her when seconds earlier he had been about to kiss her. Feeling dazed by the sudden change in him, she watched him light an oil lamp. In the bright gleam it emitted his face was expressionless, his blue eyes as cold as the Arctic winter. He took a step closer to her—reluctantly, she sensed—so that she could read his lips.

'Go and put your snowsuit on,' he instructed. 'The sky is clear, which means we shouldn't get any more snow for a few hours, and I'm going to risk making a dash down the mountain.'

Aksel could not make it plainer that he did not want to spend any more time with her than was necessary. She could not cope with him blowing hot one minute and cold the next, Mina thought angrily. Coming to Storvhal had been an impulsive mistake, and the sooner she could fly home and forget she had ever met a prince, the better.

CHAPTER EIGHT

THE JOURNEY DOWN the mountain was thankfully uneventful. The snow that had fallen earlier in the day had frozen into an ice sheet, which reflected the brilliant gleam of the moon and the countless stars suspended in the dark-as-ink sky.

Halfway down, they swapped the snowmobile for the four-by-four. As Aksel had predicted, the snow was deep in the valley, but snow ploughs had cleared the roads and eventually they reached Storvhal's capital city Jonja and saw the tall white turrets of the royal palace rising out of the dense fog that blanketed the city.

Mina turned to him. 'Why have you brought me here? I thought you were taking me straight to the airport.'

Aksel was forced to stop the car in front of the ornate palace gates while they slowly swung open. He turned his head towards her so that she could watch his lips move. 'All flights are grounded due to freezing fog. You'll have to stay at the palace tonight.'

A bright light flared outside the window. 'What the hell…?' Aksel's jaw tightened when another flashbulb exploded and briefly filled the car with stark white light. 'I hadn't expected press photographers to be here,' he growled. The gates finally parted and he put his foot down on the accelerator and gunned into the palace grounds.

'You'd better prepare yourself for the reception committee,' he told her tersely as he parked by the front steps and the palace doors were opened from within.

'What do you mean?'

'You'll see.'

As Aksel escorted Mina into the palace she understood his curious comment. Despite it being late at night, a dizzying number of people were waiting in the vast entrance hall to greet the prince. Courtiers, palace guards and household staff dressed in their respective uniforms bowed as Aksel walked past. There were also several official-looking men wearing suits, and Mina recognised the young man with round glasses as Aksel's personal assistant, Benedict Lindburg. She knew there must be a buzz of conversation because she could see people's lips moving, but it was impossible for her to lip-read and keep track of what anyone was saying.

The crippling self-consciousness that Mina had felt as a child gripped her now. She hoped no one had spoken to her and thought she was being rude for ignoring them. Instinctively she kept close to Aksel and breathed a sigh of relief when he escorted her into a room that she guessed was his office and closed the door behind him so that they were alone.

Aksel's eyes narrowed on Mina's tense face. 'I did warn you,' he said, stepping closer to ensure that she could see his mouth moving. 'It must be difficult to lip-read when you are in a crowd. At least you can charge up your hearing-aid batteries while you are at the palace.'

'What do all those people want?'

He shrugged. 'There is always some matter or other that my government ministers believe requires my urgent attention.' His life was bound by duty, but for a few moments Aksel imagined what it would be like if he were not a prince and were free to live his life as he chose, free to make love to the woman whom he desired more than any other.

Daydreams were pointless, he reminded himself. 'The fog is forecast to clear by tomorrow afternoon and a member of my staff will drive you to the airport and book you onto a flight,' he told her abruptly. 'Whereabouts in London do you live?'

'Notting Hill—but I won't go back home until the paparazzi have grown bored of stalking my flat.'

Aksel frowned. 'Do you mean you were hounded by journalists?'

'My friend Kat saw a group of them outside my front door. She won't mind if I stay with her for a few days— and hopefully the furore about my alleged affair with a prince will die down soon.' She gave him a wry look. 'Anyway, it's not your problem, is it? You are protected from press intrusion in your grand palace.'

Although that was not absolutely true, Mina acknowledged as she remembered the press photographers who had been waiting at the palace gates. She wondered if Aksel resented living his life in the public eye, subjected to constant media scrutiny. In some ways this beautiful palace was his prison, she realised.

Aksel appeared tense. 'I'm sorry your life has been disrupted. I *should* have told you who I am when we first met.'

'Why didn't you?'

He hesitated. 'You might have thought I was lying to impress you and refused to have dinner with me.'

Mina stared at his mouth, feeling frustrated that she

could not hear him. 'Would you have cared if I had refused?'

His tugged his hand through his hair until it stood up in blond spikes. 'Yes.'

Her frustration boiled over. 'Then why did you leave me alone at the cabin? You let me think you didn't want me.' She bit her lip. The memory of Aksel's rejection felt like a knife wound in her heart. It had hurt far more than when she had discovered that Dexter had lied to her, she realised with a jolt of shock. How was that possible? She had been in love with Dex, but she certainly could not have fallen in love with Aksel after two days.

The glimmer of tears in Mina's eyes made Aksel's gut twist. 'My role as prince comes with expectations that would make it impossible for us to have a relationship,' he said roughly.

'That's another thing you forgot to mention when you took me to bed.'

'*Damn it*, Mina.' He caught hold of her as she turned away, and spun her round to face him. 'Damn it,' he growled as he pulled her into his arms and crushed her mouth beneath his. He couldn't fight the madness inside him, couldn't control his hunger, his intolerable need to possess her beautiful body and make her his as she had been two nights ago.

A knock on the door dragged Aksel back to reality. Reluctantly he lifted his mouth from Mina's and felt guilty when he stared into her stunned eyes. He couldn't blame her for looking confused, when he did not understand his own behaviour. His carefully organised life was spinning out of control and cracks were appearing in the ice wall he had built around his emotions.

He knew she could not have heard the knock on the door, but the interruption had reminded him that he had no right to kiss her. He dropped his arms to his sides. 'I'm needed,' he told her, before he strode across the room and yanked open the door. His mood was not improved by the sight of his chief advisor. 'Can't it wait, Harald?' he demanded curtly.

The elderly advisor frowned as he looked past Aksel and saw Mina's dishevelled hair and reddened lips. 'I'm afraid not, sir. I must talk to you urgently.'

Duty must take precedence over his personal life, Aksel reminded himself. However much he wanted to sweep Mina into his arms and carry her off to his bed, he would not allow desire to make a weak fool of him as it had his father.

He stepped back to allow his chief advisor into the room, and rang a bell to summon a member of the palace staff. When a butler arrived, Aksel said to Mina, 'Hans will show you to your room, and tomorrow he will escort you to the airport.'

It was impossible to believe that his cold eyes had blazed with desire when he had kissed her a few moments earlier, Mina thought. She sensed that his return to being a regal and remote prince had something to do with the presence of the grey-haired, grey-suited man who was regarding her with a disapproving expression.

She was not an actress for nothing, she reminded herself. Her pride insisted that she must hold onto her dignity and not allow Aksel to see that he had trampled on her heart.

She gave him a cool smile and felt a flicker of satisfaction when he frowned. 'Goodbye, Aksel.' She hesitated, and gave him a searching look. 'I hope one day you'll realise that you can't pay for your father's mistakes for ever. Even a prince has a right to find personal happiness.'

As Aksel watched Mina walk out of the room he was

tempted to go after her and kiss her until she lost her infuriating air of detachment and melted in his arms as she had before they had been interrupted by his chief advisor. He knew she was a talented actress—so who was the real Mina? Was she the woman who had kissed him passionately a few minutes ago, or the woman who had sauntered out of his office without a backwards glance?

'Sir?' Harald Petersen's voice dragged Aksel from his frustrated thoughts. 'Benedict Lindburg has informed me that members of the press were at the palace gates when you arrived and they may have seen that Miss Hart was with you.'

'Undoubtedly they saw her,' Aksel said grimly, recalling the glare of camera flashbulbs that had shone through the windscreen of the four-by-four.

The chief advisor cleared his throat. 'Then we have a problem, sir. The Storvhalian people might overlook your affair with an actress in London, but I fear they will be less accepting when it becomes public knowledge that you are entertaining your mistress at the palace as your father used to do. Some sections of the press have already made unfavourable comparisons between you and Prince Geir. The last thing we want is for you to be labelled a playboy prince.'

Harald Petersen sighed. 'You have proved yourself to be a good ruler these past twelve years, but the people want reassurance that the monarchy will continue. For that reason I urge you to consider taking a wife. There are a number of women from Storvhalian aristocratic families who would be suitable for the role. If you give the people a princess, with the expectation that there will soon be an heir to the throne, you are certain to increase support for the House of Thoresen and ensure the stability of the country.'

'What if I do not wish to get married?' Aksel said curtly.

His chief advisor looked shocked. 'It is your duty, sir.'

'Ah, yes, *duty*.' Aksel's jaw hardened. 'Don't you think I have sacrificed enough in the name of duty? For pity's sake,' he said savagely, 'I cannot speak my son's name in public, or celebrate his tragically short life.' He felt a sudden tightness in his throat and turned abruptly away from the older man. 'I cannot weep for Finn,' he muttered beneath his breath.

When he swung back to his advisor his hard-boned face showed no emotion. 'I will consider your suggestion, Harald,' he said coolly. 'You may leave me now.'

'What are we to do about Miss Hart?' Harald said worriedly.

'I'll think of something. Tell Benedict that I do not want to be disturbed for the rest of the evening.'

The following morning, Aksel stood in his office staring moodily out of the window at the snow-covered palace gardens. He tried to ignore the sudden acceleration of his heart-rate when there was a knock on the door and the butler ushered Mina into the room.

'Are your hearing aids working?' he asked as she focused her deep green gaze on his face.

'Yes, I can hear you.' She bit her bottom lip—something Aksel had noticed she did when she was feeling vulnerable. 'Why did you want to see me? I'm about to go to the airport.'

'There's been a change of plan,' he said abruptly. 'We need to talk.'

Mina suddenly realised that they were not alone. The elderly man she had seen the previous evening was in

Aksel's office and the censure in his cold stare made her flush.

'I don't believe we have anything more to say to one another,' she said bluntly.

The older man stepped towards her. 'Miss Hart, you clearly do not understand palace protocol. The prince wishes to talk to you, and you must listen.'

Aksel cursed beneath his breath. 'Mina, may I introduce the head of my council of government and chief advisor, Harald Petersen?' He glanced at the older man. 'Harald, I would like to speak to Miss Hart alone.

'Please forgive his brusqueness,' he said to Mina when the advisor had left the room. 'Harald is an ardent royalist who worked hard to help me restore support for the monarchy after my father's death. He is naturally concerned that I should not do anything which might earn the disapproval of the Storvhalian people.'

'He must have had a fit when he saw the photographs in the newspapers of you with an actress who the paparazzi labelled the Hollywood Harlot,' Mina said bleakly.

Aksel gave her a searching look. 'Why didn't you sue the newspapers for publishing lies about you?'

'I didn't have the kind of money needed to fight a legal battle with the press, and Dexter refused to deny that we were lovers because the scandal gave publicity to the film. I hoped that the story would be forgotten—and it was until I was photographed with a prince.

'What did you want to talk to me about?' Mina hadn't expected to see Aksel again and was struggling to hide her fierce awareness of him. It didn't help that he looked devastatingly sexy in a pale grey suit and navy-blue silk shirt. She longed to reach out and touch him.

Instead of responding to her question, he said roughly, 'You look beautiful. That dress suits you.'

'I feel awful for wearing your sister's clothes without her knowledge.' She glanced down at the cream cashmere dress that a maid had brought to her room that morning. 'The maid said that my skirt and blouse were being laundered, and I could borrow some clothes belonging to your sister. I'll return the dress and shoes as soon as I get back to London.'

'Don't worry about it. Linne is often sent samples from designers, but she rarely wears any of the clothes. Cocktail dresses aren't very useful on an Arctic research ship,' Aksel said drily.

He dragged his gaze from Mina's slender legs that were enhanced by three-inch stiletto-heel shoes. She had swept her long auburn hair into a loose knot on top of her head, with soft tendrils framing her face, and looked elegant and so breathtakingly sexy that Aksel was seriously tempted to lock his office door, sweep the pile of papers off his desk and make love to her on the polished rosewood surface.

He forced himself to concentrate on the reason he had called her to his office. 'You need to see this,' he said, handing her a newspaper.

Frowning, Mina took it from him and caught her breath when she saw the photograph on the front page of her and Aksel when they had arrived at the palace the previous evening. The photo of them sitting in the four-by-four showed them apparently staring into each other's eyes, but in fact she had been focused on his mouth because at the time her hearing aids hadn't been working and she had needed to read his lips.

Her frown deepened as she read the headline.
Royal Romance—has the Prince finally found love?

'I don't understand. I know there was speculation that we are having an affair, but why would the press suggest that our relationship is serious?'

'Because I brought you to the palace,' Aksel said tersely. 'You are the first woman I have ever invited here. The press don't usually camp outside the palace gates but I should have guessed they would want to follow up the story that we are having an affair. If I had known the photographers were waiting when we came down from the mountains I would have arranged for you to spend the night at a hotel.'

It was what he *should* have done, Aksel acknowledged. But his conscience had refused to leave her at a hotel in a strange country when he knew how vulnerable she felt without her hearing aids.

Mina skimmed the paragraph beneath the headline. 'How did the journalist who wrote this know that I have recently qualified as a drama therapist?' Her eyes widened as she continued reading. 'It says here that you invited me to Storvhal so that I could help the children from the village of Revika whose fathers drowned when their fishing fleet was hit by a terrible storm.'

She lowered the newspaper and glared at Aksel. 'What's going on?'

'Damage limitation,' he said coolly. 'The palace press office released certain details about you, including that you are a drama therapist.

'I've explained that my father's reputation as a playboy prince made him deeply unpopular,' he continued, ignoring the stormy expression in Mina's eyes. 'I cannot risk people thinking that I am like him, and that you are my casual mistress. It will be better if the population believe that I am in a serious relationship with a compassionate drama therapist who wishes to help the children of Revika.'

Mina shook her head. 'I refuse to be part of any subterfuge. You'll have to give a statement to the press explaining that they have made a mistake and we are not in a relationship.'

'Unfortunately that is not an option when the photograph of us entering the palace together is a clear indication that we are lovers. Some of the papers have even gone so far as to suggest that the palace might soon announce a royal betrothal.'

Her jaw dropped. 'You mean...people believe we might get married? That's ridiculous.'

'As my chief advisor often reminds me—the country has long hoped that I will marry and provide an heir to the throne,' Aksel said drily.

'I thought you were expected to choose a Storvhalian bride?'

'I don't think the people would mind what nationality my wife is. It's true that my Russian mother was not popular, but she made it clear that she disliked Storvhal and had no time for the people she was supposed to rule with my father. Your offer to help Revika's children has gone down well in the press. The tragedy of the fishing-fleet disaster has aroused the sympathy of the whole nation and your desire to help the bereaved children appears to have captured the hearts of the Storvhalian people.'

'But I didn't offer to visit the children. You gave the press false information,' Mina said angrily. 'I mean, of course I would like to help them, but my flight to London leaves in an hour.'

'Your ticket has been cancelled. We will have to go along with the media story of a royal romance for a while,' Aksel said coolly. 'In a few weeks, when you go to New

York to perform on Broadway, we'll announce that sadly, due to the pressures of your acting career, we have decided to end our relationship.'

Mina sensed that the situation was spiralling out of her control. 'You've got it all worked out, haven't you?'

'I held an emergency meeting with my chief ministers this morning to discuss the best way to deal with the situation.'

'Had it occurred to you that I might not want to pretend to be in love with you?' she demanded coldly.

His eyes showed no emotion. 'Allowing people to think we are romantically involved could be beneficial to both of us. This afternoon we will visit the village of Revika to meet the children whose fathers were killed in the disaster. It will be a good PR exercise.'

Mina was shocked by his heartless suggestions. 'You can't use those poor children for a…a publicity stunt.'

'That isn't the only reason for the visit. I have spoken to the headmistress of the school in Revika. Ella Holmberg is enthusiastic about the idea of using drama therapy to help the bereaved children. She is concerned that without help to come to terms with their loss, they could suffer long-term emotional damage.'

'That's certainly true,' Mina admitted.

'It's also true that favourable publicity would improve your image and might make people forget the scandal surrounding your relationship with a married film director in America,' Aksel said smoothly.

'I'm not going to visit the children just to improve my image. That's a disgusting suggestion.' Mina marched over to the door. 'I'm sorry, but I'd prefer to stick to the original plan and leave Storvhal. I'm sure the press interest in us will eventually die down and I refuse to pretend that we are romantically involved. I can't bear to have my personal life made public again,' she said huskily.

'What about the fishermen's children?' Aksel's voice stopped her as she was about to walk out of his office. 'They have been desperately affected by the tragedy. I thought you said you had trained as a drama therapist because losing your hearing when you were a child gave you a special empathy with traumatised children? You told me you wanted to do something meaningful with your life—and this is your chance.' He crossed the room and stood in front of her, tilting her chin so that he could look into her eyes. 'I am asking you to come to Revika for the children's sake.'

His words tugged on Mina's conscience. She felt torn between wanting to leave Aksel before she got hurt, and sympathy for the children whose lives had been shattered by the loss of their fathers. It was possible that they might benefit from drama therapy and it would be selfish of her to refuse Aksel's request to visit the children with him.

She looked away from him and her heart thudded beneath her ribs as she made a decision that she hoped she would not regret. 'I'll come with you today to make an assessment of how best to help the children. But it's likely they will need a programme of drama therapy lasting for several months.'

Aksel gave a satisfied nod. 'There is one other thing. My grandmother has asked to meet you.' Sensing Mina's surprise, he explained. 'When Princess Eldrun saw the photograph of us in today's newspapers she was dismayed because the picture reminded her of how my father had been a playboy during his reign and an unpopular monarch. My grandmother is old and frail, and to avoid upsetting her I reassured her that we are in a serious relationship.'

'I can't believe you did that!' Mina's temper flared. 'It seems awful to lie to your grandmother, even to protect her from being upset. I've told you I don't feel comfortable with the idea of fooling people, and I can't pretend to your grandmother that I'm in love with you.'

'No?' He moved before she guessed his intention and shot his arm around her waist as he lowered his head to capture her mouth. Mina stiffened, determined not to respond to him, but her treacherous body melted as he deepened the kiss and it became flagrantly erotic and utterly irresistible. With a low groan she parted her lips beneath his, but when she slid her arms around his neck he broke the kiss and stepped back from her.

'That was a pretty convincing performance,' he drawled. 'I have no doubt my grandmother will believe that you are smitten with me.'

She blushed and clenched her hand by her side, fighting a strong urge to slap the mocking smile from his face. 'You were very convincing yourself.' She was shocked to see colour rising on his cheeks. The flash of fire in his eyes told her that he was not as immune to her as he wanted her to believe, and she was certain he could not have faked the raw passion in his kiss.

'Perhaps we won't have to lie?' she murmured.

His eyes narrowed. 'What do you mean?'

She looked at him intently and noted that he dropped his gaze from hers. 'Who's to say that a relationship won't develop between us while we are pretending to be in love?'

'I say,' Aksel told her harshly. 'It won't happen, Mina, so don't waste your time looking for something that will never exist.' He breathed in the light floral scent of her perfume and felt his gut twist. 'I'm different from other people. I don't feel the same emotions.'

'Is it because you're a prince that you think you should put duty before your personal feelings—or is there another reason why you suppress your emotions?' she asked intuitively.

The image of Finn's tiny face flashed into Aksel's mind. The memory of his son evoked a familiar ache in his chest. He equated love with loss and pain and he did not want to experience any of those feelings again.

'I don't have any emotions to suppress,' he told Mina brusquely. 'I'm empty inside and the truth is I don't want to change.'

CHAPTER NINE

SHE MUST HAVE been mad to have agreed to Aksel's crazy plan to pretend that their relationship was serious, Mina thought for the hundredth time. The only reason she had done so was because she wanted the chance to try with drama therapy to help the bereaved children from the fishing village, she reminded herself.

They were on their way to Revika and the car was crossing a bridge that spanned a wide stretch of sea between the mainland and an island where the fishing village was situated. Although it was early afternoon the sun was already sinking behind the mountains and the sky was streaked with hues of gold and pink that made the highest peaks look as though they were on fire.

But the stunning views out of the window did not lessen Mina's awareness of Aksel's firm thigh pressed up against her. The scent of his aftershave evoked memories of him making love to her, when she had breathed in the intoxicating male fragrance of his naked body. It was a relief when they arrived in the fishing village, but her relief was short-lived when she saw the hordes of press photographers and television crews waiting outside the community hall to snap pictures of the prince and the woman who they speculated might become his princess.

As they stepped out of the car Aksel slid his arm

around her waist. For a moment she was glad of his moral support but she quickly realised that his actions were for the benefit of the press. When he looked deeply into her eyes she knew it was just an act, and as soon as they walked into the community hall she pulled away from him, silently calling herself a fool for wishing that his tender smile had been real.

They were greeted by the headmistress of the school where most of the children affected by the tragedy were pupils. 'The children are pleased that you have come to spend time with them again,' Ella Holmberg said to Aksel. 'They look forward to your visits.' Noticing Mina's look of surprise, she explained, 'Prince Aksel has come to Revika every week since the fishing fleet was destroyed in the storm. Many of the children whose fathers drowned are suffering from nightmares and struggling to cope with their grief. I haven't mentioned that you are a therapist,' she told Mina. 'I've simply said that you are a friend of Prince Aksel.'

The first thing that struck Mina as she walked into the community hall was the silence. There were more than thirty children present, and many of the fishermen's widows. Their sadness was tangible and would take months and years to heal, but Mina hoped that drama therapy might help the children to voice their feelings.

To her amazement, the minute Aksel stepped into the room and greeted the children he changed from the cold and remote prince she had seen at the palace and revealed a gentler side to his nature that reminded her of the man she had met in London. In order to assess the best way to help the children, Mina knew she must first win their trust, and she was pleasantly surprised when Aksel joined in the games she organised.

By the end of the afternoon the hall was no longer silent

but filled with the sound of chattering voices, and even tentative laughter. Mina sat on the floor with the children grouped around her. 'In the next game, we are going to pretend that we are actors on a stage,' she told them. 'Instead of speaking, we need to show the audience what emotions we are feeling. For instance, how would we show that we are happy?'

'We would laugh, and dance,' suggested a little girl.

'Okay, let me see you being happy.' Mina gave the children a few minutes of acting time. 'How would we show that we are feeling angry?'

'We would have a grumpy face,' said a boy, 'and stamp our feet.'

The mood in the hall changed subtly as the children expressed anger. Many of them stamped loudly on the wooden floor and the sound was deafening, but Mina encouraged them to continue. 'It's okay to be angry,' she told them. 'Sometimes we lock our feelings inside us instead of letting those feelings out.'

On the other side of the room, Aksel felt a peculiar tightness in his throat as he listened to Mina talking to the children. She seemed to understand the helpless fury that was part of grief, just as he understood what it felt like to lock emotions deep inside. He found her depth of compassion touching, but it was part of her job, he told himself.

At the end of the session the headmistress came over to speak to Mina. 'The children are having fun for the first time since the tragedy. You've achieved so much with them after just one visit.'

'I would love to spend more time with them,' Mina said softly. 'I believe that drama therapy sessions over a few months would be very beneficial in helping to unlock their emotions.'

She glanced across the room at Aksel and wondered what feelings he kept hidden behind his enigmatic façade. He was chatting to a widow of one of the fishermen. The woman was cradling a tiny baby and she held the infant out to Aksel. To Mina's shock, he seemed for a split second to recoil from the baby. His face twisted in an expression of intense pain and although she had no idea why he had reacted so strangely she instinctively wanted to help him and hurried across the room to stand beside him.

'What a beautiful baby,' she said to the child's mother. The baby was dressed in blue. 'Would you mind if I held your son?'

The woman smiled and placed the baby in Mina's arms. She was conscious that Aksel released his breath on a ragged sigh, and, shooting him a glance, she noticed beads of sweat on his brow. She supposed that the prospect of holding a tiny baby would be nerve-racking for a man who had no experience of children—but his extreme reaction puzzled her.

The moment passed, Aksel turned to talk to another parent and Mina handed the baby back to his mother and walked back to rejoin Ella Holmberg, but she was still curious about why Aksel had seemed almost afraid to hold the baby.

Ella followed Mina's gaze to him. 'The prince is gorgeous, isn't he? Plenty of women would like to catch him, but until you came along he seemed to be a confirmed bachelor. It was rumoured that he was in love with a Russian woman years ago, but I assume that he was advised against marrying her. Prince Aksel's mother was Russian, and she was as unpopular with the Storvhalian people as Aksel's father.'

Mina's stomach lurched at the idea that Aksel had loved a woman but had been unable to marry her. Had he

come to the Globe Theatre in London to see three perfor-
mances of *Romeo and Juliet* because the story about the
young lovers whose families disapproved of their union
had deep personal meaning for him? She wondered if he
was still in love with the woman from his past. Was that
why he had never married?

'That seemed to go well,' Aksel said to Mina later,
when they were waiting in the lobby for the car to collect
them. 'You made a breakthrough with the children today.'
His expression tightened. 'Watching you with them was
really quite touching,' he drawled. 'You seemed to em-
pathise with them, but I suppose that was part of your
training to be a drama therapist.'

Aksel was struggling to contain the raw emotions that
he had kept buried for the past eight years. Shockingly,
he found himself wanting to tell Mina about Finn. But
how could he trust her? He was still undecided about
whether she had tipped off the press that she had slept
with him at his hotel in London. *Helvete*, it was possible
she had betrayed him just as his mother and Karena had
done, he reminded himself angrily.

He looked into her deep green eyes and the ache in his
chest intensified. 'Who is the real Mina Hart?' he asked
her savagely. 'You acted like you cared about the children, but maybe your kindness this afternoon *was* all an
act? After all, why should you care about them? You have
a talent for making people believe in you, and today you
played the role of compassionate therapist brilliantly. The
journalist who was reporting on your visit is convinced
that you are a modern-day Mother Teresa.'

For a few seconds Mina was too stunned to speak. 'Of
course, I *wasn't* acting. Why shouldn't I care about the
children? Anyone with a shred of humanity would want
to help them deal with their terrible loss.' Her temper

simmered at Aksel's unjust accusation. 'How dare you suggest that I was playing to the press? You're the one who thinks your damn image is so important.'

Tears stung her eyes and she dashed them away impatiently with the back of her hand. 'The person you saw today is the real Mina Hart. But who are you, Aksel? I don't mean the prince—I'm curious about the real flesh-and-blood man. Why do you hide your emotions from everyone? And what the hell happened when you were invited to hold the baby? There was a look on your face—' She broke off when his jaw tensed. 'That little baby was so sweet, but you looked horrified at the prospect of holding him. Don't you want a child one day?' She stared at his rigid face, wondering if she had pushed him too far, but she was desperate to unlock his secrets. 'How do you feel about fatherhood?'

'It is my duty to provide an heir to the throne,' he said stiffly.

'Oh, for heaven's sake!' She did not try to hide her exasperation. 'You can't bring a child into the world simply because you need an heir. I'm curious to know if you would like to have a child.'

He swung away from her as if he could not bear to look at her. *'Damn your accursed curiosity!'* he said angrily.

Mina swallowed. She had glimpsed the tormented expression in his eyes that she had seen at the cabin when she had asked him about the drawing of the baby that had fallen out of his sketch book. 'Aksel...what's wrong?' she said softly. She put her hand on his arm, but he shrugged her off.

Aksel closed his eyes and pictured Finn's angelic face on that fateful morning. How could the loss of his son hurt so much after all this time? he wondered bleakly.

He lifted his lashes and met Mina's startled gaze. 'If you want the truth, I find the idea of having a child unbearable.'

Unbearable! It was a strange word for him to have used. Mina wanted to ask him what he meant, but he strode across the lobby and opened the door.

'The car is here,' he said harshly.

He said nothing more on the journey back to Jonja and his body language warned Mina not to ask him any further questions. It was a relief when they arrived at the palace and she could escape the prickling atmosphere inside the car.

As they walked into the palace Aksel was met by several of his government ministers all requesting his urgent attention. On his way into his office he glanced back over his shoulder at Mina.

'I'm going to be busy for the rest of the afternoon. This evening we will attend a charity dinner, which has been organised by Storvhal's top businesses to raise funds for the families in Revika affected by the tragedy.'

'I don't want to go.' A note of panic crept into Mina's voice. 'I can't spend an evening in the full glare of the public and the press pretending that we are a blissfully happy couple.' She hated knowing that they would be fooling people with their so-called romance.

'Tickets for the event sold out when it was announced that you will be attending with me,' he told her. 'You can't disappoint the guests who have donated a lot of money to the disaster fund to meet you.'

Frustration surged through her. 'That's blatant emotional blackmail…' Her voice trailed away helplessly as he disappeared into his office. Benedict Lindburg, Aksel's personal assistant, noticed Mina's stricken expression.

'It's easy to understand why he's known by his staff as the Ice Prince, isn't it?' he murmured.

'That's the problem—I don't think anyone does understand him.'

The PA looked at her curiously. 'Do *you*?'

'No.' Mina bit her lip. 'But I wish I did,' she said huskily.

Half an hour before they were due to leave for the charity dinner, Mina was a mass of nerves at the prospect of facing the press who Aksel had warned her would be present. Earlier, she had decided to tell him that she would not continue with the pretence that she might be his future princess. But she had changed her mind after she had met his grandmother.

Despite being ninety and in poor health, Princess Eldrun was still a formidable lady. She had studied Mina with surprisingly shrewd eyes, before inviting her to sit down on one of the uncomfortable hard-backed chairs in the princess's suite of rooms at the palace.

'My grandson informs me that you are a therapist helping the bereaved children from the fishing community whose fathers drowned.'

'I hope, through drama therapy, to be able to help the children express their emotions and deal with their grief.'

The princess pursed her lips. 'I believe too much emphasis is put on emotions nowadays. I come from an era when it was frowned upon to speak about personal matters. Unfortunately my son Geir's private life was anything but private and his indiscretions were public knowledge. I was determined that my grandson would not follow in his father's footsteps. I taught Aksel that, for a prince, duty and responsibility are more important than personal feelings.'

'What about love?' Mina asked, picturing Aksel as a little boy growing up with his austere grandmother. 'Isn't that important too?'

Princess Eldrun gave her a haughty stare. 'Falling in love is a luxury that is not usually afforded to the descendants of the Royal House of Thoresen.' She looked over at Aksel, who was standing by the window. 'However, my grandson has informed me that he loves you.'

Mina quickly quashed the little flutter inside her, reminding herself that Aksel was pretending to be in love with her so that his grandmother did not think he was turning into a playboy like his father.

'And are you in love with Aksel?' the elderly dowager asked imperiously.

Mina hesitated. She could not bring herself to lie to the princess, but she realised with a jolt of shock that she did not have to. Like Juliet, she had fallen in love at first sight. She glanced at Aksel and her heart lurched when she found him watching her. His hard features were expressionless, but for a second she glimpsed something in his eyes that she could not define. Telling herself that it must have just been a trick of the light, she smiled at his grandmother.

'Yes, I love him,' she replied, praying that the princess believed her and Aksel did not.

Now, as she prepared to spend the evening pretending that she and Aksel were involved in a royal romance, Mina's heart felt heavy with the knowledge that, for her, it was not a charade. What if he guessed her true feelings and felt sorry for her? The thought was too much for her pride to bear. Tonight she was going to give the performance of a lifetime, she told her reflection. Somehow she must convince the press and the Storvhalian people that she was in love with the prince, and at the same time show Aksel that she understood they were playing a game, and that when she smiled at him it was for the cameras and he meant nothing to her.

A knock on the door made her jump, and her breath left her in a rush when she opened it and met Aksel's ice-blue gaze. His superbly tailored black dinner suit was a perfect foil for his blond hair. He combined effortless elegance with a potent masculinity that evoked an ache of sexual longing in the pit of Mina's stomach. That feeling intensified when he swept his eyes over her, from her hair tied in a chignon, down to the figure-hugging evening gown that a maid had delivered to her room.

'I'm glad the dress fits you,' he said brusquely.

Desperate to break her intense awareness of him, she said brightly, 'It's lucky that I'm the same dress size as your sister. I assume the dress belongs to her?'

Aksel did not enlighten her that he had ordered the jade-coloured silk evening gown from Storvhal's top fashion-design house to match the colour of Mina's eyes. 'I've brought you something to wear with it,' he said instead, taking a slim velvet box from his pocket.

Mina gasped when he opened the lid to reveal an exquisite diamond and emerald necklace.

'People believe that our relationship is serious and will expect you to wear jewels from the royal collection,' he told her when he saw her doubtful expression.

She caught her lower lip with her teeth as she turned around, and a little shiver ran through her when his hands brushed her bare shoulders as he fastened the necklace around her throat. Her eyes met his in the mirror and her panicky feeling returned.

'I'm not sure I can do this—face the press and all the guests at the party.' She fiddled with her hearing aids.

'When I'm in a crowd and lots of people are talking I sometimes feel disorientated.'

'I will be by your side for the whole evening,' Aksel assured her. Mina's vulnerability about her hearing impairment was at odds with the public image she projected of a confident, articulate young woman. Once again he found himself wondering—who was the real Mina Hart? She looked stunning in the low-cut evening gown and he wished they were back at the London hotel and he could forget that he was a prince and spend the evening making love to her.

As ever, duty took precedence over his personal desires, but he could not resist pressing his lips against hers in a hard, unsatisfactorily brief kiss that drew a startled gasp from her and did not go any way towards assuaging the fire in his belly.

'Don't bother,' he told her as she went to reapply a coat of lip gloss to her lips. 'You look convincingly lovestruck for your audience.'

For a second her eyes darkened with hurt, but she shrugged and picked up her purse. 'Let's get on with the performance,' she said coolly, and swept regally out of the door.

The fund-raising dinner was being held at the most exclusive hotel in Jonja. The limousine drew up outside the front entrance and Mina was almost blinded by the glare of flashbulbs as dozens of press photographers surged forwards, all trying to capture pictures of the woman who had captured the heart of the prince.

A large crowd of people had gathered in the street, curious to catch a glimpse of their possible future princess. 'Are you ready?' Aksel frowned as he glanced at her tense face. She took a deep breath, and he noticed that her hand shook slightly as she checked that her hearing aids were in place. Her nervousness surprised him. After all, she was a professional actor and was used to being the focus of attention.

A cheer went up from the crowd when the chauffeur opened the car door and Aksel emerged and turned to offer his hand to Mina as she stepped onto the pavement. For a second she seemed to hesitate, as if she was steeling herself, but then she flashed him a bright smile that somehow failed to reach her eyes.

'Wave,' he murmured as they walked up the steps of the hotel.

Feeling a fraud, Mina lifted her hand and waved, and the crowd gave another loud cheer. 'I can't believe so many people have come out on a freezing night,' she muttered. 'Clearly your subjects are keen for their prince to marry, but it feels wrong to be tricking people into thinking I might be your future bride when we both know that I'll be leaving Storvhal soon and we will never see each other again.'

There was no chance for Aksel to reply as they entered the hotel and were greeted by the head of the fund-raising committee, but during the five-course dinner he could not dismiss Mina's comment. He glanced at her sitting beside him. She was playing the part of his possible future fiancée so well that everyone in the room was convinced she would be Storvhal's new princess. *Helvete*, every time she leaned close to him and gave him a sensual smile that heated his blood he had to remind himself that she was pretending to be in love with him. Her performance was faultless, yet he was becoming increasingly certain that it *was* a performance and the woman on show tonight was not the real Mina Hart.

'Can you explain how drama therapy could help the

children who have been affected by the fishing-fleet disaster?' one of the guests sitting at the table asked Mina.

'When we experience a traumatic event such as a bereavement we can feel overwhelmed by our emotions and try to block them out. But when we watch a film or play, or read a book, we are able to feel strong emotions because we are emotionally distanced from the story.' She leaned forwards, and her voice rang with sincerity. For the first time all evening Aksel sensed that the real Mina was speaking. 'Drama provides a safety net where we can explore strong emotions,' she continued. 'As a drama therapist I hope to use drama in a therapeutic way and help the children of Revika to make sense of the terrible tragedy that has touched their lives.'

A nerve flickered in Aksel's jaw. How could he have doubted her compassion? he wondered. Her determination to try to help the bereaved children shone in her eyes. There was no reason for her to take an interest in a remote fishing village, but it was clear that the plight of the children who had lost their fathers affected her deeply. It was impossible that Mina was faking the emotion he could hear in her voice. It struck him forcibly that she was honest and trustworthy, but his view of all women had been warped by the fact that his mother and Karena had betrayed him. He had believed that Mina had betrayed him and spoken to the press in London, but as he looked at her lovely face he saw that she was beautiful inside, and he knew he had misjudged her.

The rest of the evening was purgatory for Aksel. For a man who had shut off his emotions, the acrid jealousy scalding his insides as he watched Mina expertly work the room and charm the guests was an unwelcome shock. With superhuman effort he forced himself to concentrate on his conversation with a company director who had donated a substantial sum of money to the Revika disaster fund for the privilege of sitting at the prince's table, but Aksel's gaze was drawn to the dance floor where Mina was dancing with Benedict Lindburg.

His personal assistant was simply doing his job, Aksel reminded himself. Benedict understood that protocol demanded the prince must mingle with the guests and make polite conversation, but Mina had looked wistful as she watched some of the guests dancing, and Ben had smoothly stepped in and asked her if she would like to dance.

Aksel frowned as he watched Benedict place his hand on Mina's waist to guide her around the dance floor. In normal circumstances he liked Ben, but right now Aksel was seriously tempted to connect his fist with the younger man's face. The circumstances were anything but normal, he acknowledged grimly. Since he had met Mina his well-ordered life had been spinning out of control.

His mind replayed the scene earlier today when he had taken her to meet his grandmother. He had been fully aware that Mina had not meant it when she had told Princess Eldrun she loved him. But hearing her say the words had evoked a yearning inside him. It was ironic that in his entire life only two women had ever told him they loved him—and they had both been lying. Karena had deliberately fooled him into believing she cared for him, while Mina had gone along with the pretence of the royal romance at his request.

He scanned the dance floor, hoping to catch her eye, but she wasn't looking at him because she was too busy laughing with Ben.

'Excuse me,' Aksel said firmly to the company director before he strode across the dance floor.

'Sir?' Benedict immediately released Mina and stepped back so that Aksel could take his place. The PA could not hide his surprise. 'Sir, the head of the National Bank of Storvhal is waiting to speak to you.'

'Invite him to dinner at the palace next week,' Aksel growled.

He stared into Mina's green eyes and felt a primitive surge of possessiveness as he swept her into his arms. Desire heated his blood when she melted against him. He did not know if her soft smile was real or part of the pretence that they were romantically involved. The lines were blurring and the only thing he was certain of was that he had never ached for any woman the way he ached to make love to Mina.

'Ben,' he called after his PA. 'Send for the car. Miss Hart and I are leaving the party early.'

'But…' Benedict met the prince's hard stare and decided not to protest. 'Right away, sir.'

'Aksel, is something wrong?' Mina's stiletto heels tapped on the marble floor as she followed Aksel into the palace and tried to keep up with his long stride. He did not answer her as he mounted the stairs at a pace that left her breathless. At the top of the staircase he caught hold of her arm and swept her along the corridor, past her bedroom and into the royal bedchamber.

Mina had never been into his suite of rooms before and her eyes were instantly drawn to the enormous four-poster bed covered in ornate gold silk drapes. The royal coat of arms hung above the bed, and all around the walls were portraits of previous princes of Storvhal. From the moment Aksel opened his eyes every morning and looked at his illustrious ancestors he must be reminded that the weight of responsibility for ruling Storvhal sat on his shoulders, she thought wryly.

She was shocked by the fierce glitter in his eyes as he tugged his tie loose and ran his hand through his hair. As far as she could tell the charity dinner had gone well, but Aksel was clearly wound up about something.

'What's the matter?' she said softly.

'I'll tell you what's the matter!' He crossed the room in two strides and halted in front of her. *'You!'* The word exploded from him.

Mina stared at him in confusion. 'What have I done?'

'I don't know.' Aksel seized her shoulders and stared down at her, a nerve jumping in his jaw. 'I don't know what you have done to me,' he said roughly. 'You've be-witched me with your big green eyes and made me feel things that I didn't know I was capable of feeling—things I sure as hell don't want to feel.'

He was on a knife-edge, Mina realised. She did not pretend to understand the violent emotions she sensed were churning inside him, but her tender heart longed to ease his torment and, with no other thought in her mind, she cupped his stubble-rough jaw in her hands and pulled his head down so that she could place her mouth over his.

He groaned and clamped his arms around her, pulling her hard against him so that she felt his powerful erec-tion nudge her thigh.

'Desire was my father's downfall. I vowed that I would never be weak like him and allow my need for a woman to make a fool of me.' He slid his hand down to her bot-tom and spread his fingers over her silk dress. 'But I need you, Mina.' There was anger in his voice, frustra-tion with himself. 'I want you more than I knew it was possible to want a woman.'

CHAPTER TEN

A SHUDDER RACKED Aksel's body. He could not control his hunger for Mina and it scared him because he had always believed he was stronger than his father.

He needed to make her understand how it was for him. That all he wanted was her body and nothing else—not her beautiful smile, or the tender expression he glimpsed in her eyes sometimes, and not her compassionate heart— he definitely did not want her heart.

'You are not your father, Aksel,' she said gently. 'The people of Storvhal admire and respect you. They think you are a good monarch—as I do. But I want to know the man, not the prince. I want you to make love to me,' she whispered against his mouth, and her husky plea destroyed the last dregs of Aksel's resolve.

Wordlessly he spun her round and ran the zip of her dress down her spine. The strapless silk gown slithered to the floor. She wasn't wearing a bra and Aksel's breath hissed between his teeth as he turned her back to face him and feasted his hungry gaze on her firm breasts and dusky pink nipples that were already puckering in anticipation of his touch.

'You are exquisite,' he said hoarsely. 'At the dinner tonight I was imagining you like this—naked except for the diamonds and emeralds glittering against your creamy skin. But the truth is you don't need any adornment, angel. You're beautiful inside and out, and I...' his voice shook '...I want to hold you in my arms and make you mine.'

The flames leaping in the hearth were reflected in his eyes, turning ice to fire. 'Will you give yourself to me, Mina?'

Her soft smile stole his breath. 'I have always been yours.' She lifted her hands and unfastened the necklace, dropping the glittering gems onto the bedside table at the same time as she stepped out of the silk dress that was pooled at her feet. 'I don't need diamonds or expensive gowns. I just need you, Aksel.'

He reached for her then and drew her against him, threading his fingers into her hair as he claimed her mouth. His kiss was everything she had hoped for, everything she had dreamed of since the night at the hotel in London. They had been strangers then, but now her body recognised his, and anticipation licked through her veins as he stripped out of his clothes. In the firelight he was a powerful, golden-skinned Viking, so hugely aroused that the thought of him driving his swollen shaft inside her made Mina feel weak with desire.

He laid her on the bed and removed the final fragile barrier of her underwear before he knelt above her and bent his head to kiss her mouth, her throat and the slopes of her breasts. The husky sound she made when he flicked his tongue across her nipples made Aksel's gut twist with desire and a curious tenderness that he had never felt before. Satisfying his own needs took second place to wanting to give her pleasure.

He moved lower down her body, trailing his lips across her stomach and the soft skin of her inner thighs before he gently parted her with his fingers and pressed his mouth to her feminine heart to bestow an intensely intimate caress that drew a gasp of startled delight from Mina.

Aksel was taking her closer and closer to ecstasy, but as Mina twisted her hips beneath the relentless onslaught of his tongue she wanted to give him the same mind-blowing pleasure he was giving her. She wanted to crack his iron control and show him that making love was about two people giving themselves totally and utterly to each other.

He moved over her, but instead of allowing him to penetrate her she pushed him onto his back and smiled at his obvious surprise. 'It's my turn to give, and your turn to take,' she told him softly, before she wriggled down the bed, following the fuzz of blond hairs that adorned his stomach and thighs with her mouth.

'Mina...' Aksel tensed when he realised her intention and curled his fingers into her hair to draw her head away from his throbbing arousal. But he was too late, she was already leaning over him, and the feel of her drawing him into the moist cavern of her mouth dragged a harsh groan from his throat. The pleasure was beyond anything he had ever known. He had never allowed any women to caress him with such devastating intimacy, and he had always held part of himself back because he could not bear to be weak like his father. The Prince of Storvhal must never lose control.

But his body did not care that he was a prince who had been schooled since childhood to shoulder his royal responsibilities. His body shook uncontrollably as Mina ran her tongue over the sensitive tip of his erection. He gripped the sheet beneath him and gritted his teeth as he fought against the tide that threatened to overwhelm him.

'Enough, angel,' he muttered, tugging her hair until she lifted her head. His hand shook as he donned a protective sheath. His usual finesse had deserted him and he dragged her beneath him, his shoulder muscles bunching as he held himself above her. He watched her green eyes darken as he pushed her legs wide to receive him, and at the moment he entered her and their two bodies became one she smiled and whispered his name, and Aksel was aware of an ache inside him that even the exquisite pleasure of sexual release could not assuage.

As Aksel drove into her with strong, demanding strokes Mina knew that her body had been made for him. She arched her hips to meet each devastating thrust, until she was teetering on the edge, and her muscles clenched in wave after rapturous wave of pleasure. At the moment she climaxed Aksel gave a husky groan and buried his face in the pillows while shudders wracked his big frame.

His few seconds of vulnerability touched Mina's heart. Her passion was spent and in its sweet aftermath she felt a fierce tenderness as she cupped his face in her hands and gently kissed his mouth.

'I don't believe you are empty inside,' she whispered.

He rolled away from her and stared up at the ornate bed drapes decorated with the royal coat of arms.

'Don't look for things in me that aren't there,' Aksel warned. 'I made love to you selfishly for my own pleasure and to satisfy my needs.'

Mina shook her head. 'That isn't true, although I think you want it to be the truth,' she said intuitively. 'I think something happened that made you lock your emotions inside you.' She hesitated. 'Are you still in love with the woman in Russia who you had hoped to marry?'

'Karena?' He gave a harsh laugh, 'God, no—my youthful infatuation with her ended when I discovered the truth about her. How do you know about Karena, anyway?'

'I don't know much. Ella Holmberg told me you had been in love with a Russian woman but couldn't marry her because the Storvhalian people would not have approved.'

Aksel sat up and raked a hand through his hair. Mina missed the warmth of his body and sensed that he was drawing away from her mentally as well as physically. She was convinced that the key to unlocking him was in his past.

Wrapping the silk sheet around her, she moved across the bed so that she could see his face. She was still wearing her hearing aids, but earlier, concentrating on numerous conversations with guests at the party had been tiring, and she found it easier to read his lips.

'What did you mean when you said you discovered the truth about Karena?' she asked curiously

For a moment she thought he wasn't going to answer, but then he exhaled heavily.

'You cannot underestimate how badly my father damaged the monarchy during his reign. As you know, it wasn't just his many affairs that caused unrest.

'My father married my mother because her family owned a mining company which had discovered huge gold reserves in Storvhal's mountains,' Aksel explained. 'Instead of sharing the discovery with his government ministers, my father made a secret deal, which allowed the Russian company to extract the gold in return for a cut of the profits. He abused his position as ruling monarch and when the Storvhalian people found out that he was stripping the country's assets they were naturally horrified.

'I did not know the full extent of my father's treachery until after his death. My mother had inherited the mining company and she hoped to win my support to continue extracting the gold. I was in a difficult position. My mother was disliked in Storvhal, and by my grandmother, but she was still my mother. I often visited her at her home in Russia, and that's where I met Karena.'

He gave a cynical laugh. 'I was a young man burdened by the responsibilities of being a prince and perhaps it was no surprise that I fell madly in love with the beautiful Russian model my mother introduced me to. It was certainly what my mother had intended,' he said harshly. 'She hoped that if I married Karena it would strengthen my ties with Russia.

'But my grandmother and Harald Petersen were afraid that the Storvhalian people would not accept another Russian princess and tried to dissuade me from marrying Karena. Harald went as far as to have Karena spied on by government agents. I did not approve of his methods,' Aksel said grimly. 'But it soon became clear that Karena had duped me and pretended to be in love with me because my mother had sold her the idea that if I married her she would enjoy a life of wealth and glamour as a princess.'

'You were betrayed by Karena and your mother,' Mina said softly. 'You were hurt by the two women you loved and it's no wonder you shut off your emotions.' Aksel must have yearned for love when he had been a child growing up at the palace with his strict grandmother, she mused. She did not think Princess Eldrun had been unkind, but she had told Mina that she had taught her grandson to put his duties as a prince before his personal feelings.

His hard face showed no emotion and she despaired that she would ever reach the man behind the mask. 'After you had learned the truth about Karena, did you end your relationship with her?'

He nodded. 'I returned to Storvhal and did not expect to see her again.'

Aksel stared into Mina's deep green eyes and wondered what the hell was happening to him. He *never* talked about his past, but it was as if floodgates in his mind had burst open, and he wanted, needed, to let the secrets he had kept hidden for so long spill out of him.

'Eight months after I broke up with Karena I went to see her in Russia.'

Mina looked at him intently. 'Were you still in love with her?'

'No.' Aksel's chest felt as if it were being crushed in a vice. He drew a shuddering breath and dropped his head into his hands. 'Karena had contacted me out of the blue to tell me she had given birth to my child. She told me I had a son.'

'*A son...!*' Mina could hear the shock in her voice. 'You have a child? Where is he?' Her heart hammered against her ribs as she tried to absorb Aksel's startling revelation. 'Does he live with Karena in Russia?'

Aksel lifted his head from his hands, and Mina caught her breath at the expression of raw pain in his eyes. 'Finn is on the mountains, beneath the stars,' he said huskily. 'I took him to the Sami reindeer-herders because they are the most trustworthy people I know. They buried him according to their traditions, and they tend to his grave when I can't get up to the cabin.'

'*His grave...*' Mina swallowed hard. 'Oh, Aksel, I'm so sorry.' Driven by an instinctive need to comfort him, she put her arms around his broad shoulders and hugged him fiercely. A memory flashed into her mind. 'The sketch of the baby at the cabin, that was a picture of Finn, wasn't it?' she said softly. 'What happened to him?'

'There is no medical explanation of why Finn died.

He was a victim of sudden infant death syndrome—
sometimes known as cot death.' Aksel took a deep breath
and inhaled Mina's delicate perfume. There was something touchingly protective about the way she had her
arms wrapped around him and it was not difficult to tell
her the secrets he had never told anyone else.

'I'll start at the beginning,' he said gruffly. 'When
I broke up with Karena I discovered that she had been
cheating on me with a Russian businessman. She assumed the baby she was carrying was his, but when the
child was born her boyfriend insisted on a DNA test,
which proved he wasn't the father. Karena knew the only
other person it could be was me, and another DNA test
showed that the baby was mine.

'But even without the test I would have recognised
that Finn was my son.' Aksel's face softened. 'He was
so beautiful, Mina. I'd never seen such a tiny human
being. He was perfect, and when I held him in my arms
I promised him I would be the best father that any little
boy could have.'

Tears clogged Mina's throat at the thought of Aksel,
whose own father had more or less abandoned him when
he had been a child, promising to be a good father to his
baby son. 'You loved Finn?' she said gently.

'More than I have ever loved anyone.' Aksel's voice
cracked with emotion. 'I asked Karena to marry me. She
was the mother of my child,' he said when Mina looked
shocked. 'I knew the marriage might not be popular in
Storvhal, but Finn was my son. More importantly, I hoped
we could put aside our differences for the sake of our son
and give him a happy childhood. Karena agreed because
she liked the idea of being a princess, but she wasn't interested in Finn. She had kept her pregnancy a secret in
case it harmed her modelling career, and once the baby

was born she went to nightclubs and parties every night.'
Aksel's expression hardened. 'One night she wanted to go
out as usual and was annoyed because it was the nanny's
night off. I was leading a double life, spending the week
in Storvhal carrying out my royal duties and returning
to Russia to see Finn at weekends. I was tired that night,
but I was still happy to look after my son. But he was
restless and cried constantly. In desperation I moved his
crib into my bedroom and when he finally settled I must
have fallen into a deep sleep.

'The next morning I was surprised that Finn hadn't
woken for his next feed and I checked the crib.' Aksel's
throat felt as if it had been scraped with sandpaper. 'At
first I thought he was asleep. But he was paler than normal, and when I touched his cheek it was cold.' His throat
moved convulsively. 'That was when I realised that I had
lost my precious boy.'

Mina blinked back her tears. She had heard pain in
Aksel's voice but his face revealed no emotion. 'Have
you ever cried for Finn?' she whispered.

His expression did not change. 'Princes don't cry.'

'Did your grandmother teach you that?'

He shrugged. 'I blame myself for Finn's death,' he
said harshly.

'*Why?* You've told me that there is often no medical
explanation for sudden infant death syndrome.'

'If I hadn't been tired and slept so deeply I might have
realised something was wrong and been able to save him.'

Mina held him tighter and rocked him as if she were
comforting a child. 'I don't believe there was anything
you could have done. Finn's death was a terrible tragedy. But because you feel guilty I bet you haven't talked
about what happened, not even to your close friends or
your grandmother.'

'No one apart from Karena, my chief advisor and the Sami herders knows about Finn. You are the only person I've told.'

'You mean…?' She broke off and stared at him. 'Don't the people of Storvhal know that you had a son?'

'Harald Petersen thought if news got out that I had fathered an illegitimate child it would prove to the Storvhalian people that I was an immoral and degenerate prince like my father. There had already been one civil uprising in the country, and to maintain peace and order I agreed with Harald to keep Finn's brief life a secret. It suited Karena because she went back to her Russian oligarch who didn't want to be reminded that she'd had a child with another man.'

Mina cupped his face in her hands and looked into his eyes. 'Oh, Aksel, don't you see? You feel empty inside because you have never been able to grieve openly for Finn. You've carried the secret that you had a son who died, and it's not surprising you blocked out your emotions that were too painful to cope with.' She hesitated. 'I want to help you to deal with the painful experiences in your past. There are various kinds of psychotherapy—'

'I don't need therapy,' he interrupted her. 'I realise you mean well, Mina, but no amount of talking about the past can change what happened or bring my son back.'

'No, but it might help you in the future to love again like you loved Finn.'

'I don't want to love. I managed for most of my life without it.' He moved suddenly, taking her by surprise as he pushed her flat on her back and rolled on top of her so that his muscular body pressed her into the mattress.

'It's a fallacy that sex can only be good if emotions are involved. I can't pretend to feel emotions that don't exist for me, but I can give you pleasure when I make love to you.'

He lowered his head and captured her mouth in a hungry kiss that rekindled the fire in Mina's belly.

'This is what I want from you, angel,' Aksel said roughly. 'Your beautiful body and your sweet sensuality, that makes my gut ache.'

Mina's breathing quickened as he ripped the sheet away from her and, after sheathing himself, ran his hand possessively down her body to push her thighs apart. His erection pressed against her moist opening and her muscles quivered as he eased forwards until he was inside her.

She wondered how he would react if she told him she loved him. With horror, probably, she thought sadly. Aksel did not trust emotions and believed he was better off without love, which meant that her feelings for him must remain a secret.

Mina was not surprised when she woke up and found herself alone in Aksel's bed, but her heart sank when she turned her head and saw he had gone. She had hoped that the night of the charity dinner the week before, when the prince had so uncharacteristically opened up to her, would be the start of a new chapter in their relationship. She had hoped that Aksel was beginning to let her into his heart, but he had got up before she had opened her eyes every morning of the past week. She sighed as she looked at the empty space on the pillow beside her.

When they made love every night it was more than just good sex. Much more. He was a demanding and passionate lover, but he was tender and gentle too, and made love to her with such exquisite care that her eyes would fill with tears and he would kiss them from her cheeks and hold her so close to his heart that she felt its erratic beat thudding through his big chest. The Viking prince had a softer side to him, but in the morning she sensed that he regretted what he regarded as his weakness and resented her for undermining his iron self-control.

The situation could not continue, she acknowledged. Every day she remained in Storvhal she became more deeply immersed in the pretence that she was romantically involved with Aksel, furthering the media speculation that a royal betrothal was imminent. The press interest was so frenzied that she'd had to stop going to the village of Revika to visit the children affected by the fishing-fleet disaster, and instead the families came to the palace so that she could continue the drama therapy sessions.

The drama sessions with the children had cemented her decision to retire from acting and become a full-time drama therapist. She hoped it would even be possible for her to work with the children of Revika again after she had finished performing in *Romeo and Juliet* in New York. But first she would have to break the news to her father of her decision to leave his theatre company.

Mina sighed. Joshua was immensely proud of the Hart acting dynasty and he had been disappointed when his older daughter Darcey had turned her back on a promising stage career to train as a speech therapist. Darcey handled their temperamental, perfectionist father better than she did, Mina acknowledged. Looking back at her childhood, she realised that she had always tried to win Joshua's approval because after she had lost her hearing she'd been afraid he would love her less than her brother and sisters. She had spent her life trying to please him, and, if she was honest with herself, she dreaded Joshua being disappointed with her when she told him she was going to leave acting.

It was amazing how parents could influence their children even when they were adults, she mused. Aksel believed he must repair the damage his father had caused to the monarchy of Storvhal, and in his efforts to prove that he was not a playboy like Prince Geir he carried the tragic secret that he had fathered a son who had died as a baby. He had been unable to mourn for Finn and his grief was frozen inside him. Mina had hoped that, having confided in her once, Aksel would feel that he could talk to her about the past, but he had never mentioned his son again and any attempts she made to bring up the subject were met with an icy rebuttal.

The sound of the coffee percolator from the next room told her that Aksel must still be in the royal suite. Usually he ate breakfast early and had already left for a meeting with his government ministers by the time she got up. Hoping to catch him before he left, Mina jumped out of bed and did not bother to pull on her robe before she opened the door between the bedroom and adjoining sitting room.

He was seated at the table, a coffee cup in one hand and a newspaper in the other. He was suave and sophisticated in his impeccably tailored suit, and with his hair swept back from his brow to reveal his chiselled features he looked remote and unapproachable—very different from the sexy Viking who had made love to her with such breathtaking dedication last night, Mina thought ruefully.

She suddenly realised that Aksel was not alone and his chief advisor was in the room. To her astonishment Harald Petersen dropped onto one knee when he saw her and said in a distinctly shaken voice, 'Madam.'

As the elderly advisor stood up and walked out of the suite she glanced at Aksel for an explanation. 'What was all that about?' Her eyes widened when she saw that the front page of the newspaper had three photographs of her wearing different wedding dresses. Closer scrutiny revealed that a photo of her head had been superimposed on the pictures of the dresses, and the accompanying article discussed what style of wedding dress the Prince of Storvhal's bride might wear if there was a royal wedding.

Mina dropped the newspaper onto the table. 'Aksel, this has got to stop,' she said firmly. 'The press are convinced that we are going to get married, and we must end the pretence of our romance. It isn't fair to mislead the Storvhalian people or your grandmother any longer.'

'I agree.' He stood up and walked over to the window to watch the snow that was drifting down silently from a steel-grey sky.

'Well…good.' Mina had not expected him to agree so readily. Perhaps he had grown tired of her and was looking for an excuse for her to leave Storvhal, she thought bleakly. Her stomach hollowed with the thought that there really was no reason for her to stay. She was staring heartbreak in the face and she was scared that all the acting skills in the world would not be enough to get her through saying goodbye to Aksel without making a complete fool of herself.

'It's time to end the pretence,' Aksel murmured as if he was speaking to himself. He swung round to face her, and his mouth twisted in a strange expression as he ran his eyes over her auburn hair tumbling around her bare shoulders and the skimpy slip of peach satin that purported to be a nightgown.

Desire ripped through him, and for a few crazy seconds he almost gave in to the temptation to carry Mina back to bed and make love to her as he longed to do every morning when he woke and watched her sleeping beside him. All week he had managed to resist, reminding himself that it was his duty to be available to his ministers during working hours. He would not be held to ransom by his desire for Mina, Aksel vowed. He would not allow his weakness for a woman to deter him from his responsibilities as monarch as his father had done.

'The reason Harald knelt before you is because, by tradition, only the wife or intended bride of the prince can sleep in the royal bedchamber,' he told her.

Mina paled as his words sank in. 'We can't allow your chief minister to think I am going to be your bride. I have to leave Storvhal.' She could not hide the tremor in her voice. 'I've received a message from my father to say that *Romeo and Juliet* will open on Broadway a week early, and rehearsals are to begin in New York next week. It's the ideal opportunity to make a statement to the press that the pressure of my career has led to us deciding to end our romance.'

Aksel's brooding silence played with Mina's nerves. 'There is an alternative,' he said at last.

She shrugged helplessly. 'I can't see one.'

'We could make the story of our royal romance real—and get married.'

She fiddled with her hearing aids, convinced she had misheard him. 'Did you say…?'

He walked towards her, his face revealing no expression, while Mina was sure he must notice the pulse of tension beating on her temple.

'Will you marry me, Mina?'

Her surge of joy was swiftly extinguished by a dousing of reality. Aksel hadn't smiled, and surely a man hoping to persuade a woman to marry him would smile?

'Why?' she asked cautiously.

He shrugged. 'There are a number of reasons why I believe we could have a successful marriage. It is evident from the press reports that you are popular with Stor-vhalian people. They admire your work with the children in Revika. I also think you would like to continue to help the children,' he said intuitively. 'You could combine being a princess with a career as a drama therapist, and I believe you could be happy living in Storvhal.' He glanced away, almost as if he wanted to avoid making eye contact with her. 'It is also true that I have shared things with you about myself that I have not told anyone else,' he said curtly.

He meant his baby son. Mina's heart clenched and she reached up and touched his cheek to turn his face towards her. 'I swear I will never tell anyone about Finn...but I truly believe you should tell the Storvhalian people about him. I don't think they would judge you or compare you in any way to your father. You are a good prince, and everyone knows it. You need to be able to grieve properly for your son and lay the past to rest, and only then can your life move forwards.'

Something flared in his eyes, and Mina held her breath, willing his icy control to melt. But then his lashes swept down and his expression was guarded when he looked at her again.

'You haven't given me an answer.'

'My answer is no,' she said gently, ignoring the voice inside her head that was clamouring to accept his offer. He had said he believed they could have a successful marriage and perhaps that meant he was willing to build on their relationship, but it wasn't enough for her. 'You listed several reasons why we should get married, but you didn't mention the *only* reason why I would agree to be your wife.'

He watched her broodingly but made no attempt to close the physical space between them. Mina told herself she was relieved, knowing that if he pulled her into his arms and kissed her she would find it impossible to resist him. But perversely, part of her wished he would take advantage of the sexual chemistry they both felt. When he made love to her she could pretend that he cared for her. But there must be no more pretence, she told herself firmly.

'Is it so important that you hear me say I love you?' he demanded tautly. 'Would your answer be different if I uttered three meaningless words?'

His cynicism killed the last of Mina's hope. With a flash of insight she realised that if she married him she would for ever be trying to please him and earn his love, as she had done with her father throughout her childhood. She remembered how desperately she had sought Joshua's praise, and how a careless criticism from him had crushed her spirit. She deserved better than to spend her life scrutinising every word and action of Aksel's in the vain hope that he might one day reveal he had fallen in love with her.

'I would only want you to say those words if they *weren't* meaningless,' she told him honestly. She walked towards the bedroom. Her heart felt as if it were being ripped from her chest but her pride refused to let her break down in front of him. 'If you'll excuse me, I need to pack and phone the airport to book a flight home.'

CHAPTER ELEVEN

BENEDICT LINDBURG ENTERED the prince's office and found Aksel standing by the fireplace, staring at the flames leaping in the hearth. 'I've arranged the press conference as you requested, sir.'

'Thank you, Ben.' Aksel's stern features lightened briefly with a ghost of a smile. 'I'll be with you in a moment.'

The PA departed, leaving the prince alone with his chief advisor. 'You mean to go ahead and make a statement, then?' Harald said tensely. 'For the good of the country and the monarchy I urge you to reconsider, sir.'

Aksel shook his head. The people of Storvhal have the right to know the truth, and my son deserves to have his short life made public. Mina's words flashed into his mind. *You need to be able to grieve properly for your son.*

'I intend to commission a memorial for Finn, which will be placed in the palace gardens.' So often he had imagined his son running across the lawn in summertime and playing hide-and-seek in the arboretum. The gardens were open to the public, and he wanted visitors to pause for a moment and think of a baby boy whose time on earth had been cut tragically short.

The conference room was packed with journalists who were clearly curious to learn why they had been called to the palace. Aksel strode onto the dais, and as he looked around at the sea of faces and camera lenses he had never felt so alone in his life. His throat ached with the effort of holding back his emotions as he prepared to tell the world about Finn. He opened his mouth to speak, but no words emerged.

Dear God! He lifted his gaze to a ceremonial sword belonging to one of his ancestors, which was hanging on the wall. The ornate handle was decorated with precious jewels including a stunning green emerald that glittered more brightly than the other gems. Aksel thought of Mina's dark green eyes and a sense of calm came over him. She'd been right when she had said he could not look to the future until he had dealt with his past. Until he'd met her, he had not cared what the future held, but now he no longer wanted to be trapped in the darkness.

He took a deep breath and looked around at the journalists. 'Eight years ago, I had a son, but he died when he was six weeks and four days old. His name was Finn... and I loved him.'

Yellow taxis were bumper to bumper all the way along Forty-Second Street, and car horns blared as Mina darted through the traffic. She stumbled onto the pavement and collided with a mountain of a man who put his arms out to catch her.

'After watching you cross the road with complete disregard for your safety, I think I'd better warn your understudy that there is a very good chance she will be playing the role of Juliet when the play opens tomorrow night.'

Mina looked up at her father. 'I've got things on my mind, and I wasn't concentrating,' she admitted.

'I've noticed,' Joshua said drily. 'You've seemed distracted during rehearsals. But I suppose it's to be expected that you're nervous about making your debut on Broadway.'

Of course her father would assume that the only thing she could be thinking about was the play, Mina thought as she followed Joshua into the theatre. He strode into his office without giving her another glance and she sensed that he had already forgotten about her. His criticism hurt, especially as she had tried hard during rehearsals to hide her misery. It seemed that she could never please her father, she thought bitterly. He hadn't commented when she had told him she was giving up acting to pursue a career as a drama therapist, but she sensed he was disappointed with her.

Joshua looked surprised when she followed him into his office. 'As a matter of fact, I'm not worried about the first night,' she told him. Her frustration bubbled over. 'Can't you see I'm upset?' Heartbroken was nearer to the truth, she acknowledged bleakly. 'You must have seen the media reports that my relationship with Prince Aksel is over.' She bit her lip. 'I understand how important the theatre is to you, but sometimes, Dad, I wonder if you care about me at all.'

Joshua's bushy eyebrows knitted together. 'Of course I care about you,' he said gruffly.

'Do you?' Mina hugged her arms around her body. She could tell her father was shocked by her outburst, but this conversation was long overdue. 'Ever since I lost my hearing I've felt that you pushed me away,' she said huskily. 'It seems like nothing I do is good enough for you.' She swallowed. 'When I became deaf, I was scared that you didn't love me as much as Darcey and Vicky and Tom. You are proud of your other children, but you've never once told me that you are proud of me.'

Joshua did not respond. Mina was sure he would insist

that he had not treated her differently from her brother and sisters, but to her shock he sank down onto a chair and sighed heavily. 'I didn't mean to make you feel that I loved you less than the others, but I…well, the truth is…' For a moment Joshua Hart, the great Shakespearean actor, struggled to speak. 'I have always felt guilty that you lost your hearing, and I thought you must blame me.'

'Why would I blame you?' she asked, stunned by her father's confession. 'It wasn't your fault that I had meningitis.'

'Don't you remember I was looking after you the night you became ill because your mother was performing in a play?' Joshua said. 'You were running a slight temperature, and I gave you some medication and intended to check on you later, but I became immersed in learning my lines. By the time your mother came home and checked on you, she realised that you were seriously ill and called an ambulance.

'If it wasn't for your mother's quick actions, you could have died,' he said thickly. 'If I had called a doctor sooner, you might not have lost your hearing. I watched you struggle to cope with your deafness and I felt eaten up with guilt and sadness that I had let you down. The specialist said that we should treat you the same as we had when you could hear and not make an issue out of your hearing impairment, but when you cried because you had been teased by the other children at school it broke my heart. I think I distanced myself from you so that you did not have to cope with my emotions on top of everything else, but I didn't realise that you thought I loved you less than your siblings.'

Mina brushed a tear from her cheek. She was astounded by her father's revelation. 'I never blamed you, Dad. I was just unlucky to fall ill, and I don't suppose the outcome would have been any different if you had called a doctor earlier. Meningitis is a horrible illness that can develop very quickly. I had no idea that you felt guilty. I thought you didn't love me because I am deaf.'

'I'm sorry I didn't show how incredibly proud I am of you,' Joshua said deeply. 'You are a brilliant actress, and I know you will be a wonderful drama therapist.' He stood up and opened his arms, and Mina flew across the room and hugged him.

'Oh, Dad, I wish I had told you how I felt years ago.' She had been afraid that her father would admit he did not love her, Mina realised. Her fear of rejection and her father's feeling of guilt had created a tension between them, but she hoped that from now on they would be more open with each other.

'What happened between you and your prince?' Joshua asked. 'He has been in the news again today. Haven't you seen the headlines?' He picked up the newspaper from his desk and handed it to Mina.

Her heart missed a beat as she stared at the picture of Aksel on the front page. He looked as handsome and remote as he had done the last time she had seen him, when she had turned down his marriage proposal and he had walked out of the royal suite without saying another word.

Benedict had accompanied her to the airport. The usually chatty PA had been strangely subdued and had called to her as she was about to walk through to the departure lounge. 'I was hoping that you might be able to understand him,' he said accusingly.

Mina had struggled to speak through her tears. 'Look after him, Ben,' she'd choked, and hurried off before she changed her mind and asked him to drive her back to the palace.

The newspaper headline proclaimed: *'Prince Faces Further Heartbreak!'*

Mina quickly read the paragraphs beneath Aksel's photo.

Prince Aksel of Storvhal has made the shocking revelation that he fathered a child eight years ago. Tragically his son died when he was six weeks old. The announcement has caused a storm of public interest in Storvhal and comes a few days after the announcement that his relationship with English actress Mina Hart has ended.

The Prince issued a statement saying he was deeply saddened by the break-up and took full responsibility for Miss Hart's decision not to marry him. He went on to say he would always regret that he could not be the man Miss Hart deserved.

'Why did you decide not to marry him?' Joshua Hart said gently. 'Don't you love him?'

'I love Aksel with all my heart, and that's why I turned him down.' Her voice shook. 'He doesn't love me, you see.'

Her father studied the newspaper article. 'Are you sure he doesn't? It seems to me that he has laid his heart on the line. Why would Aksel think that he can't be the man you deserve?'

'I didn't know he felt like that,' Mina whispered. She looked at the photograph of Aksel being mobbed by journalists who were no doubt demanding to know more about the child he had fathered. His hard-boned face showed no emotion, but there was a bleak expression in his eyes that tore on Mina's heart. He must find talking about his son desperately painful, especially as he was facing the press alone.

He had been alone all his life, she thought sadly. Brought up by his grandmother who had taught him to put duty before personal happiness, he had been rejected by both his parents and Karena, the woman he had fallen in love with soon after he had been thrust into the role of Prince of Storvhal and a life of responsibility.

It was little wonder that Aksel found it hard to open up and talk about his feelings. Perhaps he did not love her, but she hadn't stayed in Storvhal and asked him outright how he felt about her because she had been afraid that he might reject her, just as she had been afraid to confront her father and risk Joshua's rejection.

Swallowing the tears that threatened to choke her, she turned to her father. 'I've been such a coward. I have to go to Storvhal right away.' She looked at Joshua uncertainly. 'But what about the opening night of the play?'

He squeezed her arm. 'I'd better go and tell your understudy to prepare for the biggest role of her life,' he murmured.

The tall white turrets of the royal palace were barely visible through the snow storm. Winter was tightening its grip on Storvhal and by early afternoon the daylight was already fading, yet Mina found the dramatic landscape of snow and ice strangely beautiful. The car drove past a park, and the sight of children building a snowman was a poignant reminder that even as a young prince Aksel had not been free to enjoy simple childhood pleasures and he had never played in the snow or built a snowman.

Benedict Lindburg met her in the palace entrance hall. 'The prince is in his office. I didn't tell him you were coming,' he told Mina.

Taking a deep breath, she opened the office door. Aksel was sitting behind his desk and had a pile of paperwork in front of him. The light from the lamp highlighted his sharp cheekbones and the hard planes of his face. He looked thinner, she noted, and her heart ached for him.

He frowned as he glanced across the room to see who had walked in without knocking. When he saw Mina his shoulders tensed and his expression became shuttered.

'Mina! I assumed you were in New York preparing for the opening performance of *Romeo and Juliet* this evening.' Although his tone was coolly detached his ice-blue eyes watched her guardedly. He picked up a pencil from the desk and unconsciously twirled it between his finger and thumb. 'Why are you here?'

As she walked towards his desk she hoped he could not tell that her heart was banging against her ribs. But then she reminded herself that she was through with being a coward and hiding how she felt.

'My father has released me from my contract with his theatre company and I've handed the role of Juliet over to another actress.'

Aksel looked shocked. 'Why would you turn down the chance to star on Broadway? Surely it's the opportunity of a lifetime that every actor aspires to?'

'I have different aspirations,' she said steadily. 'I hope to make a career as a drama therapist, but more importantly, I've changed my mind about marrying you—and if your offer is still open I would like to be your wife.'

The pencil between his fingers snapped in half and the lead tip flew across the desk.

'Why the change of heart?' he demanded. 'I thought you needed to hear a declaration of my feelings before you would accept my proposal.' Aksel's jaw tensed. 'I have to warn you that my feelings haven't changed.'

For a second her courage nearly deserted her, but for some reason she remembered the snowman in the park and her resolve strengthened.

'Nor have mine,' she said huskily. 'I fell in love with you the moment we met.'

'Mina, don't!' He jerked to his feet and strode around the desk. 'I don't want you to say things like that.' He raked his hair back from his brow and she noticed that his hand shook. The tiny indication that he felt vulnerable moved Mina unbearably.

'That's too bad, because I refuse to keep quiet about my feelings for you any longer.' She lifted her hand to his jaw and felt the familiar abrasion of blond stubble against her palm. 'I love you, Aksel. I know you can't say the words, and maybe you never will, but I don't believe you are empty inside. You were hurt, and you're still hurting now, especially since you have spoken publicly about your son.

'I can't imagine how painful it must have been for you to lose Finn,' she said gently. 'I hope that being able to talk about him will help to heal the pain in your heart, and I want to be beside you, to support you and to love you with all my heart.'

For a moment he gave no reaction. His skin was drawn so tightly across his cheekbones that his face looked like a mask, but as she stared at the rigid line of his jaw Mina suddenly realised that he was far from calm and in control of his emotions. His eyes glittered fiercely, and she froze as she watched a tear cling to his lashes and slide down his cheek. 'Aksel—don't,' she whispered, shaken by the raw pain she saw in his eyes.

'Oh, God!—Mina.' His arms closed around her and

held her so tightly that the air was forced from her lungs. 'I love you so much it terrifies me.'

His voice was ragged and she could hardly hear him, but she watched his lips move and her heart felt as though it were about to explode.

'I couldn't bear to lose you. It would be like losing Finn all over again,' he said hoarsely. 'I convinced myself that I would be better off not to love you. I thought that if I denied how I felt about you the feelings would go away.' He rubbed his cheek against hers, and Mina felt a trickle of moisture on his skin.

'I didn't want to love you,' he whispered. 'But when you left I felt like someone had cut my heart out, and I had to face the truth—that I will love you until I die, and without you my life is empty and meaningless.'

He drew back a fraction and looked down at her. 'I planned to wait until *Romeo and Juliet* had finished its run on Broadway, and then come and find you and try to persuade you to give me another chance.' He brushed away the tears on her cheeks with his thumb pads. 'Does the thought of me loving you make you cry, angel?'

'Yes, because I know how hard it is for you to speak about your feelings,' she said softly. 'You were taught to put your duties as a prince before your personal happiness.'

'The night in London and the time we spent together when you came to Storvhal were the happiest times of my life. I have never met anyone as caring and compassionate as you, but I told myself I could not trust you because it made it easier to deny my feelings for you.' Aksel's throat moved convulsively. 'You were right when you guessed that I had buried my grief about Finn, but you gave me the guts to face up to the past and tell the Storvhalian people about my son as I should have done years ago.'

He dropped his arms from her and walked around his desk to take something out of a drawer. Mina caught her breath when he came back and opened the small box in his hand. The solitaire diamond ring glistened like a tear drop, like the bright stars that watched over the mountain where his baby son rested.

'Will you marry me, my love, and be my princess? Will you walk with me all the days of our lives and lie with me all the nights, so that I can love you and cherish you with all my heart for ever?'

She gave an inarticulate cry and flung her arms around his neck. 'Yes—oh, yes—on one condition.'

Aksel searched her face and felt that he could drown in her deep green eyes. 'What condition, angel?'

'That, as soon as our children are old enough, we will teach them to build a snowman.'

He understood, and he smiled as he slid the diamond onto her finger. 'We'll also tell them how much we love them every day. Out of curiosity, how many children were you thinking we should have?'

'Four or five—I'd like a big family.'

'In that case—' he swept her into his arms and carried her out of his office, heading purposefully towards the stairs that led to the royal bedchamber '—we'd better start practising making all those babies.'

Aksel glanced over the bannister at his PA, who was hovering in the hall. 'Ben, I'd like you to draft an announcement of the imminent marriage of the Prince of Storvhal to Miss Mina Hart, who is the love of his life.'

Benedict Lindburg bowed and surreptitiously punched the air. 'I'll do it immediately, sir.'

On Christmas Eve the bells of Jonja's cathedral rang out in joyful celebration of the marriage of the Prince of

Storvhal and his beautiful bride. Despite the freezing temperature, a vast crowd lined the streets to watch the candle-lit procession of the prince and princess as they travelled by horse-drawn carriage to the palace where they hosted a feast for five hundred guests, before they left by helicopter for a secret honeymoon destination.

Mina wore her white velvet wedding dress for the short flight to the cabin in the mountains. She carried a bouquet of white roses and dark green ivy, and wore a wreath of white rosebuds in her hair.

'Have I told you how beautiful you look, my princess?' Aksel murmured as he lifted her into his arms and carried her into the cabin. 'You took my breath away when you stood beside me at the altar and we made our vows.'

'To love and to cherish, till death do us part,' Mina said softly. 'I meant the words with all my heart, and I will love you for ever.'

Aksel kissed her tenderly, but as always their passion quickly built and he strode into the bedroom and laid her on the bed. 'You could have chosen to spend our honeymoon at a luxury hotel anywhere in the world,' he said as he stripped out of his suit and began to unlace the front of Mina's dress. 'Why did you want to come here to this remote place?'

'It's the one place where we can be completely alone.' Mina caught her breath as he tugged the bodice of her wedding gown down and knelt over her to anoint her dusky pink nipples with his lips.

He smiled. 'Just the two of us—what could be more perfect?'

'Well…' She took his hand and placed it on her stomach. 'Actually—there's three of us.'

She held her breath as emotion blazed in his eyes, sadness for the child he had lost that turned to fierce joy as the meaning of her words sank in.

'Oh, my love.' Aksel's voice cracked as he bent his head and kissed her still-flat stomach where his child lay. 'As I said—what could be more perfect?'

* * * * *

MILLS & BOON®

Maybe This Christmas

Author of *Sleigh Bells in the Snow*

Sarah
Morgan

Maybe this
Christmas

COMING SOON
OCTOBER 2014

* cover in development

Let Sarah Morgan sweep you away to a perfect
winter wonderland with this wonderful Christmas
tale filled with unforgettable characters, wit,
charm and heart-melting romance!
Pick up your copy today!

www.millsandboon.co.uk/xmas